'Are you all demanded.

For several secon beating, all the tiny hairs on the back of her neck shivering to attention. Slowly she raised her eyelids, unwilling to believe what she was hearing. It had been over three months since she'd last heard that voice but it had haunted her mercilessly.

After all her efforts at tracking him down had failed in Italy she had believed that she would never know who he was. It was impossible that he should suddenly step into the same lift. . .and on today of all days.

'You!' she breathed as her eyes finally focused on the tall dark-haired man in front of her. 'Dr da Cruz.'

Josie Metcalfe lives in Cornwall now with her long-suffering husband, four children and two horses, but, as an Army brat frequently on the move, books became the only friends who came with her wherever she went. Now that she writes them herself she is making new friends and hates saying goodbye at the end of a book—but there are always more characters in her head clamouring for attention until she can't wait to tell their stories.

Recent titles by the same author:

WORTH WAITING FOR
LOUD AND CLEAR
FORGOTTEN PAIN
BOUND BY HONOUR
A VOICE IN THE DARK
SEEING EYE TO EYE
HELL ON WHEELS
SECRETS TO KEEP
NO ALTERNATIVE

FOR NOW,
FOR ALWAYS

BY
JOSIE METCALFE

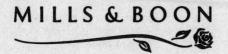

MILLS & BOON, the Rose Device and
LOVE ON CALL are trademarks of the publisher.
Harlequin Mills & Boon Limited,
Eton House, 18-24 Paradise Road, Richmond, Surrey TW9 1SR

© Josie Metcalfe 1996

ISBN 0 263 79856 9

Set in Times 10 on 12 pt. by
Rowland Phototypesetting Limited
Bury St Edmunds, Suffolk

03-9610-46356
Made and printed in Great Britain

CHAPTER ONE

'WHEN will the pain end. . .?'

Leo sat down heavily on the edge of the luxurious king-sized bed and, lifting the glass to his lips, threw the contents to the back of his throat. He grimaced at the unaccustomed taste even as he welcomed the fiery bite of it sliding down.

With a rock-steady hand he poured another generous inch into the hand-cut crystal, not appreciating the quality of the glass or the brandy in his search for anaesthesia.

'Here's to you, Andreas, with my grateful thanks,' he toasted his absent friend with the beautiful glass which had accompanied the expensive brandy to his hotel room, hardly noticing the gleams struck from the facets by the last rays of the dying sun as he sent the contents swiftly after the first dose.

He reached for the jacket of his silvery grey suit, dragging it towards him across the bed with no regard for the excellence of the tailoring.

'Where is it. . .?' he muttered as he fumbled one-handedly for the inside pocket to retrieve his wallet, letting the jacket drop heedlessly to the floor between his feet as he flipped the dark leather open to slide out a small photograph.

A sad smile barely lifted the corners of his mouth and came nowhere near his steely grey eyes.

'Happy birthday, Nico,' he whispered as he traced

the smiling face with a trembling finger and a solitary
tear slid down his cheek.

Maria couldn't remember when she'd ever felt this
tired. Not even during the nightmare years of her training had a week piled on the agony like this.

The taxi lurched round the corner, almost seeming
to tilt onto two wheels before the driver began weaving
in and out of the other traffic again, the oncoming
headlights glaring into eyes already sore from lack of
sleep and at least one bout of weeping.

As her purse slid off her lap and on to the floor,
Maria grabbed for the door-handle just in time to prevent herself joining it.

'Please, God,' she murmured through gritted teeth,
nearly at the end of her tether. How she was supposed
to be able to concentrate in the morning if she didn't
get to the hotel soon, she didn't know, but there was
no way she could have made the right flight; no way
that she could have left any earlier when Cara had
needed her there. . .

As they finally drew up outside the entrance to the
hotel she surreptitiously crossed her fingers that her
room would still be available in spite of her late arrival.

She dredged up a tired smile for the rather flustered-
looking elderly man behind the desk, knowing that she
looked less than her best. Her skin felt sticky and
shiny and she could tell that her dark hair had begun
to straggle untidily down the back of her neck.

'Good evening.' She deposited her suitcase gratefully at her feet. 'My name is Maria Martinez. I'm
terribly sorry I'm so late but. . .'

'*Scusi, Signorina. Non parla inglese.*' He was

shaking his head dolefully, his large dark eyes making him look almost like one of those toy dogs she sometimes saw in the back windows of cars.

'And I don't speak Italian. . .' For a moment Maria was astounded that a hotel of this size would have staff on Reception who couldn't speak English and then she dragged her concentration back to her predicament. Her shoulders slumped as she tried to cudgel her tired brain into life.

It took several minutes of pantomime and the comparison of the name in her passport with the list of reservations he held at the counter before the penny seemed to drop and he let loose with a barrage of Italian that hit her aching head like bullets from a machine-gun.

The only sense she could make of it all was that the room she had booked was no longer available but, if she didn't mind, there was another one she could have elsewhere in the hotel.

At least that was what she hoped he was saying.

When he seemed to be trying to tell her that there was some problem with this other room, too, she hastily held both hands up as she shook her head.

'No problem. No problem,' she assured him, too tired to try to work out what he was saying and too tired to care, even if he was offering her the broom cupboard. All she needed was somewhere to sleep before she fell down where she stood.

'*Grazie.*' She murmured the sum total of her Italian vocabulary as she hastily scribbled her name in the register and prepared to follow him to the lift.

When she finally managed to shut the door on his voluble attempts at a further explanation Maria slumped back against its welcome support and blearily tried to focus.

'Wow,' she breathed, her tired eyes widening in disbelief as she surveyed her sumptuous surroundings. 'Talk about luxury. . .' Her gaze slid from the mouldings on the ceiling, highlighted by the subtle positioning of the peach-shaded lamps, to the acres of thick cream carpet.

The bed itself must have been nearly the size of her whole flat back in England and just the sight of the mountain of soft peach-coloured pillows was enough to make her yawn.

She deposited her solitary suitcase on the ornate stand at the foot of the bed and flipped the lid open to retrieve her washing kit, stumbling as she kicked off her shoes on the way to the bathroom.

With a mental apology to her foster-mother for the untidy pile of clothing she dumped beside the shower she climbed under the soothing stream. For several minutes she allowed the warm water to pound the stiffness out of her neck and shoulders before she shampooed her long hair with practised ease and rinsed her body off.

She didn't have the energy to do much more than towel-dry the dark mass and run a wide-toothed comb through it, even though she knew that she was encouraging it to revert to its natural wild curliness.

A quick glance confirmed the fact that she'd forgotten to bring her nightdress to the bathroom with her but she couldn't focus her concentration enough to worry about it.

'The hotel's warm enough for me not to catch a cold and I'll sort my hair out properly in the morning,' she mumbled around her toothbrush.

Within seconds she was reaching out to turn off the light as she opened the door to her room.

'Oh.' She paused in the darkness, her hand searching for the light switch while she strained her eyes to get her bearings. 'I don't remember turning the lights out. . .'

Catching sight of the corner of the bed in the gloom, she gave up her quest for the switch and padded silently across the velvety soft carpet.

The covers appeared to have been turned back in her absence and she felt a momentary pang of guilt for the poor maid who'd had to stay on duty so late before she slid bonelessly under the covers.

Maria just had enough time to be grateful that her exhaustion would enable her to sleep in spite of the events of the day before the world faded into oblivion.

She must have been sleeping very deeply because the dream slid so gently into her mind that she wasn't aware of the beginning. . .

She knew that she felt warm and comfortable, the way she had the first day she'd met her new foster-mother and had been swept up against Anna Martinez's pillowy bosom in a loving hug. She'd been seven years old and it had been the first time that she'd ever remembered anyone wanting to hold her. . .

This dream was different because she wasn't wearing the slightly dingy pink dress which was all the orphanage could find to fit her tall thin body. This time she wasn't wearing any clothes at all but instead of feeling cold she felt warm. . .as warm as if she was curled up in front of a fire with the flickering fingers of firelight playing over her shoulders and arms and warming her breasts.

'Mmm,' she murmured her approval as she stretched out and arched as languidly as a basking cat to allow the heat to play over the rest of her body. 'Nice. . .'

The fire was getting hotter, even seeming to reach inside her, spreading, growing fiercer and wilder until her whole body turned to searing liquid—like molten lava consuming everything in its path as the volcano erupted.

Maria drifted in strange peace after the explosion, for the first time feeling totally content and without a trace of the lingering loneliness which had always permeated her life.

'Thank you.'

The sound of the husky voice in her ear was enough to drag her out of her drowsy lethargy and back to full consciousness in a hurry. Every muscle tensed in terror, her horrified eyes flying wide open to stare blindly into the darkness trying to see the owner of that voice— trying to see whose body was pinning hers to the bed.

This *wasn't* just a dream brought on by exhaustion; this was really happening to her. There was a man in her bed and she had no idea who he was or what he was doing there. . .

'Oh, God, thank you. . .'

Her frantic thoughts scattered as his husky heartfelt words were followed by the gentle touch of his lips tracing the outline of her features with the delicacy of butterfly wings.

'You'll never know how much this means to me.' There was such agony in his deep voice that Maria paused even as she braced her fists against the powerful male body looming over her in the darkness, the frantic scream trapped in her paralysed throat.

'Sometimes it feels as if the pain will go on for ever. . .as if I'll never escape the memories. . .' His husky voice broke on that desolate note, the spicy heaviness of expensive brandy on his breath playing over her face as she felt his fingers spear through her hair and fan it out across the pillow.

'So silky,' he whispered in a wondering tone. 'So healthy and full of life. . .' His hands traced the shape of her head, his fingertips hesitantly outlining the curves of her eyebrows and cheek-bones before he slanted his mouth over hers in a kiss of such stunning sensuality that Maria was mesmerised, hardly able to remember why she had been prepared to fight him.

All she knew was that in his words, in the very tone of his voice, she had heard all the agony of emptiness and loneliness that she felt inside.

In the end the only thing that counted was that he shared the same pain as she did. It didn't seem to matter that she was going against a lifetime's convictions— all she wanted to do was comfort him and draw consolation in return.

Instinctively she uncurled her hands to run her fingers through his curls and over the warm, smooth skin of his chest and up around his neck, exploring the warmth and strength of the powerful muscles and the heavy silk of his thick hair.

Her tentative response drew an answering groan from deep in his throat. Convulsively his powerful arms wrapped around her and she delighted in the physical contact after the emptiness of this awful day.

Fleetingly she remembered the situation that she'd dragged herself away from back in England.

It had been little comfort to the grieving parents to

know that everyone had done their best for their beautiful daughter. Maria knew, intellectually, that it was true. But she also knew that it was her emotional response to losing a favourite patient that was turning her inside out; that, in spite of everything she'd been able to do for Cara, her frail body hadn't been able to take any more.

Despite all their antibiotic armoury Cara hadn't had the reserves to fight off that last overwhelming infection. . .

'Sometimes it seems as if death always wins. . .' she whispered through an aching throat as she wrapped empty arms around him and relished the comfort of a warm male body against hers, strong and full of life.

'Not always,' he vowed. There was desperation in his tone as he gathered her tightly against himself. 'Sometimes life is too compelling to deny. . .'

This time Maria knew where the searing heat was coming from; knew that the touch of his hands and his body on hers were an undeniable primitive force—an affirmation of the triumph of life over death which turned her to liquid fire until all she could do was hold him tight as the world exploded around them.

'I've overslept!'

Maria sat bolt upright in the middle of the bed, her heart pounding furiously as she tried to sort out her frantic thoughts.

She was in Italy to take part in a conference and if she didn't get moving she'd be late for the presentation of the first paper.

She'd swung her feet over the side of the bed and taken several steps towards the *en suite* bathroom before the subtle aches in her hips and thighs brought the memories of what had taken place last night flooding over her.

She stopped in her tracks as if she'd hit a brick wall and swung round to stare back at the bed.

'Oh, my God!' Her hands came up to cover her horrified mouth as she took in the rumpled state of the bedclothes.

The fact that half of the sheets were hanging off the side of the bed could have been put down to a bad night's sleep but the imprint of a second head on the pale blue pillows was something that she couldn't ignore.

'Who. . .? Where. . .?' Her eyes feverishly examined every corner of the room and her brain didn't know which question it wanted answered first.

This wasn't her room.

She gazed at the pale, mossy-green carpet and the blue draperies accenting the room. The décor was just as opulent but the colour scheme was totally different.

Her heart was racing unevenly as she searched for some evidence of what had happened during the night. She *knew* that it had happened; knew that she had contributed to the disarray of that luxurious bed with a man she'd never seen.

There was no time to check around the room but, as far as she could see, he didn't seem to have left anything behind. There was certainly no note and not a trace of his belongings—nothing to suggest who he had been or where he had gone.

Heat seared her cheeks as she realised that in the dark of the night she had shared the most intimate of delights with a stranger and she wouldn't even recognise him if he stood in front of her.

The sound of a car horn somewhere outside the hotel window brought her back to her present concerns as she glanced at her watch.

'Oh, no!' she wailed as she dived towards the bathroom. 'Five minutes to go. . .'

Her shower was so swift that the water hardly had time to land on her body before she was switching it off. There wasn't time to do anything with her hair except drag a comb through it and subdue it at the back of her neck with an ornate clasp and she had the feeling that her face would never need blusher again. . .

This time she took note of the fact that there were two doors leading into the bathroom and left by the one which took her back to the peaches-and-cream room she remembered from last night and the familiar suitcase waiting at the foot of the pristine bed.

'Where have you been?' Lena Harper hissed when Maria finally slid into the empty seat beside her. 'You've missed the first session completely.'

'I can't have!' Maria muttered to her colleague as she checked her watch. 'I'm only ten minutes late.'

'Add an hour,' she was advised wryly. 'You forgot to change your watch.'

Maria groaned and rectified her mistake immediately.

'What did I miss?' she demanded under her breath while she tried simultaneously to listen to the venerable gentleman who was reading an introduction to a slide presentation. 'What did he cover in the first session?'

'Not him. It was Leo da Cruz. Thalassaemia,' her friend supplied cryptically.

'Damn,' she swore under her breath as she realised that she had missed one of the key presentations she had wanted to attend. 'Was he good? Did you manage to get any notes?'

'Superb in a very intense kind of way. He's very much into early diagnosis and counselling. . .' There was a brief delay as the lights were dimmed and Lena took advantage of it to flick back several pages in her spiral-bound notepad to show Maria the notes she'd taken. 'I'll let you have what I've got at the next break.'

The first slide flicked up onto the giant screen at the front of the specially appointed conference room and as the professor began to point out the salient features Lena and Maria turned their attention towards the purpose of their attendance.

By the time they joined the stream of people making their way towards the dining-room they were deep in a discussion of what they'd seen, hardly noticing the press of bodies around them as they reached for trays and filled them with food from the selection available.

Maria was halfway through her meal before she had the uncanny feeling that someone was staring at her. The fine hairs at the back of her neck began to prickle as they stood on end in the classic warning of danger.

'Do you know any of the other delegates?' Lena broke into Maria's distracted thoughts.

'Apart from the names of some of the people presenting papers, I don't think so,' she frowned quizzically, her fork halfway to her mouth. 'Why?'

'Are you certain? Only Leo da Cruz has been watching you ever since he sat down.'

'Has he?' Maria blinked. 'Which one is he? Perhaps he's miffed that I missed his lecture this morning.' She allowed her eyes to scan the section of the dining-room she could see but didn't immediately recognise anyone.

Suddenly her gaze was caught by a pair of steely grey eyes set under frowning dark brows. A strange shiver slid its way along her spine, lifting all the hairs to attention as she was trapped by their intensity, almost unable to drag herself away.

'Do you know him?' Lena's voice broke into the frozen tableau and the spell was broken.

'Who?' Maria's brain seemed to be moving at half-speed.

'Leo da Cruz,' Lena repeated in an exasperated tone as though she was talking to a particularly dim-witted child.

'Which one is he?' She gratefully seized the opportunity to look around the rest of the room, careful not to let her eyes meet a certain pair of steely grey lasers.

'Obviously you don't know who he is or you'd know that Leo's the gorgeous one with the dark curly hair,' Lena teased as she nodded towards the very table that Maria had been carefully avoiding looking at.

'H-he was the first speaker this morning?' She was certain that Lena would see through her pathetic attempt at nonchalance, especially as she had no idea why she was reacting in this way. It wasn't as if she was totally unfamiliar with the fact that men found her attractive and she could hardly have gone through all her years of medical training without learning how to cope with the occasional brush with male appreciation.

. . . Except, somehow, *his* interest didn't seem quite like appreciation. Maria was strangely aware that in spite of the fact that he appeared to be observing her like a cat watching a mouse he didn't seem to be regarding her as juicy prey.

There was more than a hint of disapproval in his attitude towards her and she wondered if Lena had any idea why.

'Lena. . .?'

'Are you sure you haven't met him?' the older woman interrupted as she murmured out of the corner of her mouth, a familiar matchmaking gleam in her dark eyes. 'He certainly seems to be interested in you.'

'Lena!' She felt the heat rise in her cheeks as she prayed that her friend's voice hadn't carried as far as the other table. 'It's all very well joking like that back on our own turf but you could end up embarrassing everyone if we're overheard here! What if he's a married man? You could start all sorts of rumours with comments like that.'

'He's not married; he hasn't been tamed yet,' Lena continued incorrigibly. 'You mark my words. You'd better be ready because he'll make a move on you before the conference is over.'

Maria wasn't certain whether the sudden leap in her pulse was as a result of anticipation or trepidation at the thought of being confronted at close quarters by a man with such a powerful presence. Lena was certainly right about the fact that he didn't look tame. . .

What if he was the man in the room next door? The thought flashed through her brain like a lightning strike as her eyes fixed helplessly on his handsome face.

She felt the colour leave her face as she frantically traced his features one by one. Was that the thick silky hair that she'd run her fingers through? Were they the cheek-bones she'd explored——the lips she'd kissed?

Was that the powerful body that she'd held in her arms and allowed—no, actively *encouraged*—to perform intimacies that she'd never known before?

'I'm sorry,' she gasped as she stumbled to her feet. She couldn't bear to stay under his stern grey gaze for another minute, especially when there was a chance that he might be the one who. . . 'I. . .I left something in my room. I'll see you in a minute. . .' and she fled from the dining-room, desperate to get to the suite.

The lifts were all occupied when she reached them but she couldn't face waiting in the small group. The emotions inside her were so strong that she felt that the whole world must be able to read them on her face.

Until she had herself under control again she needed to be alone so she whirled towards the stairs and sped swiftly up the first flight until she was out of sight at last.

For a second she thought she could hear an echo of the deep voice she'd heard in the dark of the night but she shook her head violently and started up the next flight of stairs, concentrating on putting one foot in front of the other until she was finally able to shut her door behind her.

There was a fatal fascination in the way her eyes were drawn towards the connecting bathroom and she was powerless to prevent her feet taking her in that direction.

Would the room on the other side still be as empty as it had been when she'd left it this morning or would *he* be there? Perhaps, this time, the door would be locked so that she would never find out who the mysterious stranger was. . .

She hesitated in the quiet coolness of the bathroom,

her hand hovering fearfully over the doorhandle for several long seconds before she silently turned it.

The door swung easily on well-oiled hinges and the sight that met her eyes made Maria draw in a sharp breath.

The room was pristine. Everything looked as fresh and clean as if it was new—as if it had never been used at all, never mind as recently as last night.

She was shaking her head as she slowly backed out of the bathroom, pulling the door shut again and turning the key.

She knew, now, that there was no point in trespassing any further into the other room. If there had been any evidence to point to the identity of the man who had slept there last night the very efficient chambermaid would have removed it while Maria had been attending the conference.

Suddenly the enormity of the situation hit her as she realised for the first time the possible long-term consequences of what had taken place.

Her legs were trembling as she sank down onto the edge of the bed that she should have occupied alone last night and she clasped her hands together tightly on her lap to still the nervous fidgeting of her fingers.

As she'd never had the time nor the inclination to indulge in any form of promiscuity she'd never needed to worry about such things as contraception or 'safe' times. Now, with the speed of a bullet, her armour had been shattered and she was left trying to remember whether, in the heat of unexpected passion, her lover had thought to take any precautions of any sort.

Her lover. . .

Maria's shudder was partly due to the unwilling

arousal that her memories brought with them and partly the result of self-disgust that she could have behaved in such a thoughtless way. She knew better than to take stupid risks with her precious health. . .

Think. . .! She sank her teeth into her bottom lip as she tried to cudgel her brain into action.

The most important thing was to find out the name of the man who had shared the other half of this very luxurious suite last night. Without his name she had no way of asking those vital questions.

Unfortunately she also needed to find a way to make her enquiries without anyone knowing why she wanted the information. In spite of the more relaxed attitude towards doctors' private lives, if so much as a hint of what had happened last night became public knowledge it could still have disastrous repercussions on her professional reputation.

Maria waited impatiently until the rest of the delegates were all on their way towards the conference suite before she approached the reception desk. She was dreading the difficult task she would have in making herself understood if the day staff were as ignorant of English as the elderly man had been last night.

'May I help you, madam?' The young man at the desk smiled whitely as he pronounced the attractively accented words and she breathed a sigh of relief.

'I wonder. . . Could you tell me who is occupying the other half of the suite I'm in? They seem to have left some things in the bathroom and. . .' She bit her tongue as it threatened to run away with her. She never had been able to look someone in the face and tell a lie.

'And your name, madam?' He turned towards the hotel register.

'Martinez. Maria Martinez. I've come here for the conference. . .'

'Ah, yes. You're in room number. . . No. . .' His eyebrows drew together as he bent forward to decipher the writing.

'I arrived late last night,' Maria volunteered helpfully. 'There was an older gentleman at the desk but I'm afraid I don't speak any Italian and I couldn't understand what he was saying. . .'

'My father,' the young man smiled widely. 'He came in to sit at the desk while I took my wife to hospital. We had a baby boy last night.' There was immense pride in the pronouncement and Maria couldn't help congratulating him on their good fortune.

'As for your room—' he finally remembered the reason for their conversation '—my father has written the new number of your room against your name but there is no one occupying the other half of the suite.'

'Not today,' Maria agreed. 'But last night there was a man. . .someone who left some things in the bathroom. . .' It was so frustrating having to think carefully about every word in case she gave any hint of what had happened.

'There is no record of anyone being in that room for the last couple of days, madam,' he said soothingly. 'If the room is going to be empty for a while now I'll get the chambermaid to check the bathroom and remove anything which shouldn't be there.' He smiled again, his teeth very white in his darkly tanned face. 'I'm sorry if you've been inconvenienced.'

'But. . .' Maria realised that there was no point in

pursuing it any further. 'There's no urgency,' she smiled wanly. 'Tomorrow morning when she comes to clean the room will be soon enough.'

In spite of the importance of the conference Maria was unable to concentrate properly for the rest of her stay, every fibre strained by the tension that filled her.

It seemed as if every few minutes her mind would return to the well-worn groove as she tried to solve the problem of finding out who the stranger was.

It seemed impossible.

She wasn't even able to take any pleasure in the fact that Lena's prediction had come to nothing.

'Well,' her motherly colleague was still trying to justify herself as they boarded their return flight together. 'I still say he would have approached you if he hadn't had to leave the conference early.'

Maria laughed. She'd been so concerned with her failure to find out the identity of her mystery man that she'd almost forgotten Lena's words.

She made a joking reply as she settled back in her seat ready for take-off but was surprised to feel a lingering disappointment that she hadn't had a chance to meet the elusive Leo da Cruz.

In the last few years he had become something of an authority on the diagnosis and treatment of inherited haematological diseases and it would be at least another year before she could reasonably expect to hear him speak at such a conference again.

The thought of next year's events stopped her thoughts in their tracks. Who knew where she would be by then or what she would be doing? It would all depend on what happened in the next few weeks.

CHAPTER TWO

'MARIA!'

The sharp concern in the voice was the only thing which helped her to hang on to consciousness as she gripped the edge of the desk, a piece of paper crackling against her clammy palm.

'I've got you.' The words coincided with an arm wrapped around her shoulders. 'You can let go now.'

Maria concentrated on releasing her fierce grasp on the desk and sank gratefully onto the chair which nudged the backs of her legs. She didn't think her shaky legs could have held her up much longer.

'Don't tell me this damn flu has got you, too.' Peg Mulholland's voice surrounded her as she sat with her eyes tightly closed. 'You look dreadfully white. I think you'd be better off at home.'

'No,' Maria whispered when she realised that shaking her head only made the ache worse. 'Ian Stanton didn't make it in last night so I ended up working straight through and then. . .' She stopped abruptly as her hand tightened convulsively around the piece of paper and she felt the cold sweat beading her forehead.

'Well, you're in no fit state to stay here,' Peg said decisively, the caring side of her nature showing through.

Maria heard the familiar sound of the buttons on the telephone then listened while her friend organised for a taxi to be ready for her in fifteen minutes.

23

It wouldn't have been so bad if it had been a quiet night. She could have coped if she'd been able to snatch a few hours' sleep just to recharge her batteries but there'd been no time for that.

Within hours of each other there had been an admission from a car crash to set up on traction after Orthopaedics had finished patching him up and drips and analgesia to regulate in the sterile side ward for two young burns victims from a house fire.

She'd never managed to work out why it always seemed to take ten times longer to get everything organised at night when they were trying not to disturb the rest of the patients already on the ward.

Then, when she finally thought she could curl up and close her eyes, one of her special patients had spiked a temperature during a blood transfusion and she'd spent several hours sitting beside her bed to keep her company while her mother snatched some sleep.

'Are you feeling faint?' Peg's voice demanded. 'If it's safe to leave you I'll get your things and the porter can bring you a wheelchair.'

'No.' Maria's voice sounded rusty as she forced the sound through her dry throat. 'I'll be all right in the lift.' She pushed herself up in the chair, straightening her shoulders and lifting heavy lids. There was nothing to be gained by giving in to the overwhelming load that had landed on her shoulders. The only thing she could do was what she had *always* done—grit her teeth and keep going.

'You look as if a puff of wind would blow you away,' Peg frowned. 'Are you sure it isn't this bug?'

'I'm sure,' Maria smiled wanly. 'I'll go straight to bed when I get home and sleep the clock round. I'll be better by the morning.' She couldn't meet Peg's eyes, certain that a ward sister with her experience would be able to tell that her near collapse had been caused by something far worse than mere tiredness. Would she be able to detect the guilt and shock which Maria was sure must be written across her face?

'Well, you'd better not come anywhere near my ward if you aren't in better shape tomorrow,' Peg warned sternly. 'I can't have you giving things to my patients.'

'It isn't anything contagious.' Maria was seized with the desire to laugh wildly at the thought then felt the ominous prickle of tears building up behind her eyes. 'I'm sorry to leave everyone in the lurch like this. Can I get you to notify the appropriate administrators?'

'Of course you can,' Peg agreed briskly. 'You just concentrate on taking yourself out of here and getting some sleep.'

Maria slumped back in the corner of the lift and closed her eyes, mentally counting the floors as she waited for the quiet ping which would tell her that she'd arrived at the ground floor.

She was only halfway there when the lift slid to a halt and the doors swished open to admit someone else into her quiet space. The best way she'd found to discourage conversation was to avoid making eye contact so she kept her eyes tightly closed and waited for the journey down to continue.

'Are you all right?' a deep voice demanded and for several seconds Maria's heart seemed to stop beating, all the tiny hairs on the back of her neck shivering to attention. Slowly she raised her eyelids, unwilling to believe what she was hearing. It had been over three months since she'd last heard that voice but it had haunted her mercilessly.

After all her efforts at tracking him down had failed in Italy she had believed that she would never know who he was. It was impossible that he should suddenly step into the same lift. . .and on today of all days.

'You!' she breathed as her eyes finally focused on the tall dark-haired man in front of her. 'Dr da Cruz.'

She'd never been able to forget those steely grey eyes boring into her that day at the hotel but she'd never dreamed that they belonged to the tortured soul she'd held in the night.

'Dr Martinez,' he nodded curtly. 'Is there somewhere we can talk?'

'Talk?' Maria echoed weakly.

'Are you on your way to the staff canteen? Perhaps I could get you something to eat.' There was a frown on his face as his glance slid over her as though he disapproved of the weight she had lost in the last three months.

'No, I'm not. . . I mean. . .' Her stammered reply was halted by the final jerk as the lift arrived on the ground floor.

'Come,' he ordered as he grasped her elbow firmly in one lean hand and drew her out of the path of the people trying to enter the small space, leading her towards the cafeteria which the hospital provided for visitors.

'I'm on my way home,' Maria objected as she tried to pull her arm out of his grasp. 'I've got a taxi waiting for me outside.'

'So much the better,' he pronounced as he altered

direction and marched her towards the entrance doors. 'We can share the taxi.'

'I. . . But. . . You. . .' Maria spluttered in his wake but she might as well have saved her breath for all the notice he took.

It wasn't until he released her to open the door that she was able to stand her ground.

'We can't share the taxi,' she said fiercely, all too aware of the interested gaze of a group of staff leaving the hospital at the end of their shift. She knew just how quickly gossip could spread in their enclosed world. 'Everyone will think that I've invited you to come home with me.'

'We shared more than a taxi in Italy,' he growled in a low voice as he leant towards her. 'The least you can do is allow me to apologise for. . .for what happened.'

To Maria's astonishment she saw a tide of dusky red wash over the lean planes of his cheeks and she was certain that she was witnessing a rare occurrence.

'Please?' his dark lashes lifted suddenly and she was speared by the brilliance of his gaze. 'I need to speak to you. To explain.'

She hesitated only briefly before she nodded her agreement and ducked inside the waiting vehicle, sliding all the way across the seat to leave a space between them when he joined her. Even in her exhausted state she was aware of the electric current which seemed to pulse between them and she knew that it was imperative that she kept a clear head. Too much depended on it.

'Alma Road,' he directed the cabbie and Maria drew in a sharp breath.

'How did you know where I live?' she demanded, an uncomfortable feeling settling in the pit of her stomach.

'I asked your colleague, Lena Harper,' he said with a reminiscent frown. 'She seemed only too willing to tell me—as if she'd been expecting me to ask.'

The words were almost an accusation and Maria subsided into a guilty silence.

Now it was her turn to feel the heat build in her cheeks as she remembered Lena's knowing looks and her prediction that the good-looking doctor was interested in her.

The fact that she wasn't speaking didn't mean that her brain wasn't working. Questions were multiplying in her head faster than the flu virus currently decimating her colleagues but before she could sort them out into any kind of coherent order the taxi was drawing up in front of the house where she rented the ground-floor flat.

'Have you got your key?' He paused with one foot on the doorstep and held out his hand.

'I'm perfectly capable of opening my own door, thank you.' Maria fixed him with a steady gaze, the key held tightly in her hand. She had the instinctive feeling that the next few minutes were going to be very uncomfortable and she needed to feel that she had some measure of control over the situation.

With a brief nod he conceded and stepped aside to allow her to reach the door and followed her into the flat.

'Would you like a drink?' Maria walked straight through towards her compact kitchen, desperate to have something to occupy her hands. She'd always thought that the hallway of her little domain was pleasantly spacious but as soon as she closed the front door she had the impression that there wasn't enough air to breathe.

At a shade under six feet and with a slim, agile build,
it wasn't the size of her visitor that made the space
seem crowded; it was the powerful presence of a man
driven by silent demons which was making her flee.

'I've got tea or coffee,' she called over her shoulder.
'I don't think there's anything stronger—I only have
brandy in at Christmas. . .' She bit her tongue but it
was too late. The memory of the taste of brandy in his
kisses must have been so close to the surface of her
mind that the words came out by themselves.

'Coffee will be fine, thank you.' He paused, then
added quietly, 'I very rarely drink alcohol.'

The flat tone of his voice drew her eyes towards
him in time to see his mouth twist in a grimace of
self-disgust. 'I don't suppose that's something you find
easy to believe after our last encounter.'

Maria was silent while she finished placing their
cups on a tray but her mind was busy. Finally she
turned to face him, her chin raised just a little higher
than usual.

'Actually, I would find it very easy to believe,' she
said as she met his combative gaze calmly. 'I think you
were under a great strain for some reason and had a
little more brandy than you should. If I hadn't come
into your room by mistake you'd have slept it off with
little more than a hangover to show for it.'

She turned away and drew in a shaky breath before
she picked up the tray and led the way through to her
tiny lounge.

As she settled herself in her favourite armchair she
had time to marvel at the resilience of the human body.
An hour ago she had been so tired that she was close
to collapsing. A hefty shot of adrenaline in the shape

of Dr da Cruz and she was even alert enough to cross swords with him.

'Thank you for your generosity.' The deep voice interrupted her musing as he lowered himself onto one end of the settee and reached for his cup. 'Not many women would be so calm about what happened.'

Maria hoped that her shrug conveyed nonchalance. There was no way she was letting him know how desperately she had wanted to find out who he was and how frustrating it had been not to be able to find out.

First she had been blocked by the hotel manager's insistence that the room had been unoccupied and then there had been her concern that she would only be drawing attention to what had happened if she'd asked him to check further. . .

'Tell me,' he began, 'why didn't you say anything when you saw me the next day?'

'Because I didn't know who you were,' she replied, puzzled by his question.

'Do you mean to tell me you were waiting for a formal introduction?' His laugh was incredulous.

'No,' she drew in a calming breath, 'I mean, I had no idea who you were.'

'Your friend knew,' he pointed out. 'I heard her tell you my name.'

'But she didn't know what had happened the night before and I didn't know that you were the person in the other room.' Her patience was becoming a little frayed. She wasn't accustomed to having her word doubted. 'I did try to find out who it was but the hotel didn't seem to have any record of anyone being booked there that night.'

His steely grey eyes travelled over her face as though

he could see inside her head, and she didn't like the vulnerable feeling that his intensity caused.

'Is it my turn to ask a question?' She relinquished her cup and wove her fingers together on her lap as she turned the spotlight on him. 'If you knew who I was, why didn't *you* say something the next day?'

'Because. . .' He hesitated, his dark eyelashes sweeping down to hide his eyes from her for a moment before he continued, almost belligerently, 'Because I thought you'd been paid to come to my bed.'

'What. . .?' For several seconds Maria couldn't breathe with the shock of his words. She could feel the colour draining from her face and her eyes grew impossibly wide. 'How *dare* you suggest such a thing about me? I'm not a. . .I would never. . .'

'Please!' His own cup clattered as he hurriedly deposited it on the tray. 'I *know* it isn't true now.'

'What do you mean? ''Now''?' Indignation made her voice rise. 'It's *never* been true.'

'But I only found out a few days ago when I caught up with Andreas.'

'And who's Andreas? Your pimp?' She poured scorn into the word as the acid of betrayal ate away at her. How dared he think that she would stoop to such a thing? She was no prostitute—to be paid for her favours. . .

'He's the friend who supplied me with the brandy that night.' He hurried into speech as though he knew what course her thoughts were taking. 'Then, when I turned over in the middle of the night and I found you next to me in the bed, I thought he'd arranged that, too. Look—' he sat forward on the edge of the settee '—as soon as I found out that I'd completely misread the situation I set out to track you down.'

'Why?' Maria was deliberately blunt. 'If you didn't think it important enough to speak to me the next morning why bother to look me up now?'

'Firstly because I wanted to apologise.' He was strangely vulnerable in his embarrassment, unable to meet her eyes. 'As you've gathered, I'd had too much to drink and I know I don't hold alcohol well. I was afraid. . .I didn't know how. . .forceful. . .I was. I doubt that I was capable of much finesse. . .' His words died away as he gazed down at his hands linked together between his knees, the colour darkening over the tanned skin of his cheek-bones.

No finesse? Maria could have laughed aloud. Even on a bad performance it seemed that this man could exceed all her wildest fantasies about sex. . . And he'd been worried about it. . .

'No,' she murmured, her own cheeks flaming at her vivid memories of the pleasure he had brought her. 'You weren't too forceful.'

'I'm glad,' he said softly. 'I would have hated for you to think that I didn't appreciate. . .'

'Please!' If her face grew any hotter she would burst into flames. 'You said there was another reason why you came. . .'

'I just wanted to reassure you that you didn't have to worry that you might have caught anything from me.' There was a gravelly tone to his voice. 'I hadn't been with a woman since. . .for a couple of years so you were quite safe.'

There was a grim irony to his words and for a moment Maria contemplated asking him to explain. But that would imply that she was willing to tell him her own secrets and she couldn't face that yet. The realisation was too new—too fresh to reveal to someone who was, after all, little more than a stranger.

Suddenly her tiredness returned with full force and her eyelids felt weighted with lead. With her brain function slowed to near zero, she knew that she wasn't fit to cope with the problems that talking to him would cause. Not today.

'I'm sorry, Dr da Cruz,' she began as she dragged herself to her feet.

'Leo,' he prompted as he stood up effortlessly and offered her a helping hand. 'I'm sorry we had to have such a traumatic first meeting, especially as we're bound to be running into each other.'

'Are we?' Maria blinked owlishly.

'Specialising in the same field, it seems inevitable.' He smiled briefly and Maria blinked again at the difference the change in expression made to his face. 'Especially,' he continued, 'over the next year or two while I'm based just a few miles down the road. . .'

With those innocent-sounding words he'd delivered a bombshell.

Maria's pulse began thudding uncomfortably at the base of her throat as she contemplated the difficulties which could arise if she kept bumping into Dr da Cruz—Leo—for the next couple of years. There was no way that she could avoid seeing him—not if she wanted to take advantage of his expertise in their special field. Her shoulders slumped as she caught a glimpse of the scale of the problems ahead of her.

'I'm sorry, Dr. . .I mean, Leo. I'm dead on my feet; I've got to get some sleep.' She rubbed both hands over her face.

'I'll leave you in peace, then.' He led the way to her door, turning back towards her at the last moment just as she reached out to release the catch.

Suddenly they were mere inches apart, her eyes on a level with the mobile perfection of his lips as he opened his mouth to say goodbye and a strangely intimate silence grew between them.

'Maria?' The huskiness in his voice drew her eyes up to meet his. 'I'm sorry we met the way we did but I'm not sorry that we met.' She watched as his gaze flicked from her eyes to her mouth and back again and she felt the heat as clearly as if he'd touched her. Her own fingers ached to trace the features that she'd only known in darkness and she had to clench her hands into fists inside her pockets to make sure that she didn't succumb to temptation.

There was a subdued crackle as she found the piece of paper that she'd deposited in one pocket before she left the hospital and suddenly she remembered what was written on it.

She didn't know whether he expected her to say anything further but her head was so full of the knowledge of what was contained on that piece of paper that it was empty of words. She contented herself with a nod of acceptance as she finally opened to door for him.

'I'll be back in a couple of weeks,' he said as he stepped out onto the front path. 'A semi-official invitation to visit your department.'

Through the racing thoughts filling her head Maria vaguely remembered being told about the visit. At the time she had thought of it as a golden opportunity to ask the questions she'd never had a chance to in Italy but now the whole significance of that had altered, too.

'We've been looking forward to it.' She managed to dredge up a polite smile for him but the effort needed to maintain a calm front was getting greater every minute.

'I'll see you, then.' He gave a mock salute and finally set off down the road.

Maria pushed the door shut and leant back against it, her legs so rubbery that it almost felt as if she'd had the bones removed.

Slowly she took the piece of paper out and smoothed it carefully between her fingers to flatten the creases—not that she needed to read the words to know what it said. The message was burned into her brain for ever.

It had taken months for her to finally admit that there was something wrong with her since her trip to Italy but with her steady weight loss the lab result was last thing that she had expected.

'Pregnant,' she whispered, the thought still enough of a shock to set her pulse racing as she looked down at the too-slender flatness of her body. 'I'm over three months pregnant.'

'He's arrived.' Ian Stanton beamed as Maria stuffed her heavy coat in her locker. 'The whole department is in a flap. The poor nurses are just about falling over their feet trying to be helpful!'

'What on earth for?' Maria demanded crossly. 'He's only a man. It's what's inside his head that's important.'

She dragged a comb through the straggly mess the wind had made of her hair and swiftly subdued it into a tight coil at the nape of her neck. A quick glance in the mirror showed her that her pasty complexion was paler than ever. It could do with a liberal application of blusher and some lipstick to make her look as if she was at least halfway alive but she refused to take the time to do it.

'He'll only think I did it for his benefit,' she muttered under her breath, knowing, deep inside, that he would have been right.

It had been a full month since she'd last seen Leo da Cruz, his visit having been postponed twice in the interim, and she was very much aware that the time hadn't been kind to her.

She'd heard that some women sailed through pregnancy glowing with health and energy but you couldn't prove it by her. The intermittent nausea which had eventually led to the discovery of her condition hadn't gone away when she'd completed her first trimester. In fact, it seemed to have worsened. Even her dark, honey-coloured eyes seemed dull when set in a face that looked permanently grey and drained.

She compromised over her refusal to resort to cosmetics by biting her lips and pinching each of her cheeks but the effects, while they lasted, left her looking like a badly painted doll.

The only good thing about her poor health, she thought wryly as she made her way towards the paediatric ward, was the fact that she was now halfway through the pregnancy and her condition was still unnoticeable enough to be a secret between herself and her obstetrician.

As she half turned to shoulder her way through the first set of double doors she pushed her hands into the pockets of her fresh white coat so that the unbuttoned edges were drawn together as a form of camouflage.

'Good morning, Doctor.' Peg Mulholland looked up

to greet her from the bedside closest to the door as
Maria closed the child-proof doors behind her. 'If you'd
like to go straight through Dr da Cruz is in my office
waiting for you.'

Maria raised her hand in acknowledgement, knowing
that Peg would be joining them as soon as she had
finished supervising the junior nurse's work.

Meanwhile she altered direction, swallowing hard
and drawing in a deep, steadying breath before she
entered the room.

He hadn't heard her come in and for several seconds
she was able to gaze down on the closely trimmed,
thick, dark curls on the head angled towards her as he
concentrated on the paperwork spread out on the desk
he'd appropriated.

'Good morning, Dr da Cruz,' she said quietly as she
sat herself in one of the extra chairs which had been
brought through for this initial meeting.

She smiled inwardly as he jumped with surprise at
the unexpected sound of her voice and looked up.

'Maria?' The smile he wore when his eyes met hers
faded slowly as his gaze travelled swiftly over her. 'My
God, what have you done to yourself? Have you been
ill?' He straightened up out of the chair so fast that it
scraped noisily over the floor and rocked back onto the
back legs before righting itself.

'What's happened? Have you seen a doctor? Are
you fit enough to be at work?'

By the time he had finished firing questions at her
he had circled the desk and had reached the other side
of the room, dropping suddenly to one knee beside her
so that he could look at her more closely.

Maria found the proximity almost suffocating and

couldn't stop herself leaning away from him in spite of the fact that her first impulse had been to throw herself into his arms.

'I'm fine,' she said, her voice sounding too quiet when heard through the thunder of her pulse. 'The hospital's had a particularly nasty flu bug going round. . .' She shrugged one shoulder as though that half-answer was enough to explain her pale face and limp hair and the fact that she could count her ribs in the mirror of her bathroom.

'At a guess you've been filling in for sick colleagues and then conveniently forgetting to take time off for your own recovery,' he hazarded. 'You look as if you could do with a large meal and a week's sleep.'

'I'd heard Italian men were good at sweet-talking women but I don't think that's quite what they meant,' she teased, hoping that the humour would persuade him that she was well.

'Perhaps it doesn't work when only half of you is Italian,' he returned as he straightened up again, the smile he gave her not entirely hiding his concern.

'And which half is that?' She drew in a surreptitious breath of relief that he was putting a little more space between them.

'The half that isn't Greek.' The smile was wider that time.

'So, how much of you is English?' She frowned at the mathematics.

'None of me.' He held his hands away from his sides. 'Before you you see a pure-bred Mediterranean mongrel.'

Their wary laughter was interrupted by the arrival of the rest of the group and their meeting got under way.

'...With co-operation between our various disciplines—' Leo was drawing the hour-long discussion to a close '—we can look forward to the time when not only are all babies routinely checked for sickle cell disorders at birth, so that parents can be informed and proper follow-up arranged, but all mothers are routinely checked for the disorders during pregnancy to pick up any who don't know that they are at risk.'

'One of the difficulties with population migrations is that many people these days don't know what their genetic inheritance is because they don't know where their ancestors came from,' one of the registrars commented. 'You can't tell just from a person's colouring whether they're from a high-risk Eastern European background with excellent spoken English or whether they're low-risk English with a taste for foreign holidays and suntans.'

There was a round of laughter but they all knew that he'd pointed out a valid problem.

'I sometimes think the American idea of having to have a blood test before you can apply for a marriage licence is a very good idea,' one of the midwives commented. 'Except, of course, not everyone waits until they're married before they start producing children.'

'In the end it all comes down to the individual,' Maria contributed. 'We can take the blood tests and tell the parents that they're both carriers of, for example, sickle cell trait and arrange counselling. If they then decide to take the one-in-four risk of having a child with the disease we can do the various tests up to the twentieth week of the pregnancy to find out if it's a sufferer.

'But, even if we find out that the child has inherited

sickle cell disorder, it's still the parents' choice if they want to continue with the pregnancy.'

The meeting broke up soon after that but her thoughts were still on Marco, her little brother who'd been born with the form of sickle cell disorder called beta thalassaemia major.

'You're looking sad.' The deep voice spoke softly beside her and Maria looked up to discover that they were the last two left in the room.

'I'm sorry. That was very rude of me.' She avoided looking at him by concentrating on closing her notepad and capping her pen. 'My mind must have wandered.'

'It didn't seem like a very happy thought. . .' His tone invited her to explain but it was something that she was wary of speaking about. She still became emotional, even after all this time.

'Just some old memories,' she said as she dredged up a smile. 'Sometimes I make the mistake of allowing the work I do to become too personal.'

'I don't think anyone can avoid it when they're work-ing with children,' he said quietly. 'Especially something potentially lethal such as the sickle cell dis-orders. From the first moment of conception the child is doomed to go through years of pain and medical intervention, with some form of limitation on nearly every aspect of their lives.'

'It doesn't all have to be doom and gloom,' Maria objected. 'With the advances in early diagnosis and improved blood transfusion, and especially now that we can remove the accumulated iron, many of them can lead a nearly normal life. Many of them are going on to marry and. . .'

'*Normal*,' he scoffed, unexplained bitterness colouring his voice. 'I sometimes wonder if they would agree? If they knew that they could have been spared the unremitting pain of the condition, let alone the treatment—all the transfusions, all the injections and medicines and all the restrictions. Would they have preferred their parents to have terminated the pregnancy? Would it be fairer if they'd never been born?'

CHAPTER THREE

MARIA was very subdued during the rest of her shift.

She still managed to smile for her patients, cheering up their newest patient by drawing happy faces on the plaster casts immobilising both of her broken legs.

'Have you thought of names for them?' she queried with a serious expression.

'Names for what?' Five-year-old Jemma was mystified.

'For your casts, of course,' Maria replied as though the answer was obvious. 'You can't moan about them if you haven't given them names. How will they know which one you're telling off?'

As she continued on her way around the ward she left a more cheerful child trying out the names of her favourite television characters to see which she preferred—and a pair of very bemused parents.

'Hello, Dr Maria,' piped up a cheeky young voice from the next bed. 'I'm beating Hussein this time. Look.'

Hassan Rehman's big dark eyes beamed up at her, his hand clutching one of the controls for the computer game they were playing.

'No, you're not,' his identical twin brother denied from the next bed. 'You cheated when the nurse was checking the blood.'

Hassan and Hussein were two of her regular patients: eight-year-olds whose thalassaemia meant that they

42

had to come in regularly each month for transfusions of washed, packed red cells to correct their anaemia.

Just a few minutes in their lively company was enough to reinforce her feelings that the life of a child with beta thalassaemia was far from the gloomy prospect that Leo had painted.

As she glanced back at the two of them on her way out of the ward she was determined that she was going to introduce them to him at some time before they were due to go home later in the afternoon.

She was just reaching out her hand for a plate of salad when a familiar sandalwood fragrance warned her that Leo was there just before he spoke.

'You'll never put weight on with that.' One lean, tanned hand reached past her for the roast meal on offer and tried to slide it onto her tray before she could put the salad there. 'This would give your system something to fight back with,' he advised.

When Maria turned to let him know that she was perfectly capable of choosing her own meals she caught a look of open concern on his face and was so surprised that the sharp words remained unspoken.

'I haven't got my appetite back yet.' She made her explanation vague, aware that his weren't the only ears which could be listening.

'Will you give it a try if I entertain you while you eat as much as you can manage? You'll never keep the pace up without cracking if you don't get a bit more meat on your bones.'

'That depends what you mean by "entertain".' She chose her words carefully for maximum effect. 'Do you sing or dance? Perhaps you tell jokes?'

'Smart alec,' he muttered in her ear as he reached

for a large glass of orange juice with one hand and her elbow with the other, escorting her across to the table where his own food waited.

'Ah!' Maria smiled, the bubble of pleasure that he was going to be eating with her lifting her spirits. 'I hadn't realised this was an invitation to dine out in style. . .!'

She managed to eat half of the meal in the time he cleared his own plate before she suddenly remembered the Rehman twins.

'Leo, have you got a few minutes free this afternoon?' She crossed her fingers surreptitiously under the edge of the table. 'Or have the powers that be managed to arrange back-to-back meetings right through?'

'Let me check.' He slid a clipboard across the table towards himself. 'Any particular time?'

'Before six o'clock this evening?' She knew the twins' parents would be coming to collect them at that time so it would be too late for her purposes.

'It looks as if I'm getting some time off for good behaviour at about five-thirty. Was it something special you wanted me to see?'

'Yes,' she smiled secretively. 'Very special. But I'm not giving you any hints.'

The rest of the afternoon flew by with a full out-patients clinic to attend and the usual mountain of paperwork to complete before she could hurry back up to the ward.

'Right on time.' His deep voice reached her as she released the child-proof catches and he followed her through the doors and into the ward.

'As you know,' Maria prefaced his visit with a brief

résumé, 'we already do a sickle cell check on every patient who comes in for surgery in case of problems with anaesthetics and cross-matching and we also check all pregnant women and their newborns.'

'And your counselling service is absolutely first-rate,' he commented approvingly. 'If only there were more like it. . .'

'We also see a number of children with the various sickle cell disorders on a regular day-care basis for blood transfusions and when they have crises and we teach their parents how to cope with setting up the drugs regimen at home. Also, with the advent of bone marrow transplants. . .'

She watched as his expression changed, the smile almost disappearing as his eyes took on the pained expression that she'd seen before.

'Leo—' she paused and reached out her hand spontaneously to touch his wrist '—I know your specialisation means that you've seen far more of the problems than I have and I know there are some cases where the children go through hell but, you must admit, they're far fewer these days. . .'

She stopped, knowing that all the words in the world wouldn't have the impact of the Rehman brothers. 'Come with me,' she invited and led the way across the ward.

'Hassan. Hussein. I would like you to meet Dr da Cruz.'

Two pairs of identical dark eyes swung away from the electronic mayhem they were creating to look up at him, their ready smiles as broad as ever.

'Hi.' It was cheeky Hassan who spoke first. 'Are you Dr Maria's boyfriend?'

'Hassan!' Hussein's horrified voice broke in before Maria could find her tongue.

'I don't know,' Leo countered, managing to sound suitably worried. 'Do you think she'd like me to ask her out?' Maria saw the sly wink he shared with the two boys, drawing attention to her rapidly pinkening cheeks. 'She's very pretty, isn't she?'

'She's *beautiful*,' Hassan corrected Leo then tilted his head to one side in a considering way. 'I don't know if she'd go out with you, though. She might not have time. She has to look after all us kids cos we're special.'

'Why are you special?' His smile told Maria that he was enjoying his encounter with these pint-sized charmers.

'Because——' Hussein took over the conversation '——we're some of her regular customers.' He rolled the syllables around on his tongue as though he enjoyed using the phrase.

'That's cos we have to have blood transfusions,' the irrepressible Hassan butted in, pointing up to the IV stands at the sides of their beds. 'We've both got beta thalassaemia.'

Maria watched as Leo's smile dimmed but there was no time for the fact to register with her charges as their parents arrived just then.

'Dr Martinez.' Mr Rehman greeted her with a smile. 'How have they behaved today? Are you desperate to get rid of them yet?' He tousled their thick dark mops of hair affectionately.

'They've been good as gold,' she confirmed. 'In fact, I've just been introducing them to Dr da Cruz who's a specialist in sickle cell diseases.' She stood back to

allow them to shake hands and watched as the
Rehmans' open pleasure in their sons and their continued good health worked their own special magic
on Leo.

It wasn't until the nurse came to remove the IVs that
Maria caught sight of the clock on the wall at the end
of the ward.

'Look at the time!' she exclaimed, grabbing Leo's
sleeve. 'You're supposed to be going to another meeting in a minute, aren't you?'

'And you're supposed to be going off duty,' he
responded with a meaningful glance at his watch. 'It
looks as if you're just as poor a timekeeper as I am and
we're both going to be late.'

There was a smiling round of farewells and promises
to 'see you next month' from the two boys as the family
left the ward and then they were left standing together
just outside the double doors.

'Well. . .' Maria clenched her hands into fists inside
her pockets '. . .I suppose you'd better be on your way
to your next meeting. Where is this one?'

'That rather depends on you,' Leo said quietly.

'Me?' Maria's voice came out as an undignified
squeak.

'I'm hoping I can persuade you to have dinner with
me.' He paused as a visitor walked past them to let
herself through the double doors into the ward.

'Well, I suppose there hasn't been very much time
for the two of us to discuss the ramifications of. . .'

'Maria. . .' The single word silenced her frantic bab-
ble and she bit her lip as their eyes met. 'I don't want
to have a business meeting; I want to take you out for
a meal.'

'Why?' The word came out as a breathy whisper as her heart caught in her throat.

'Several reasons.' He settled his shoulders against the wall as though he was prepared to stay as long as it took to persuade her, one foot nonchalantly crossing over the other. 'First, as those imps in there said, because you're a beautiful woman and, second, because I enjoy your company but mostly because we haven't had anything to eat since that cafeteria meal at lunchtime and I'm starving but I don't like to eat alone. . .'

He attempted to look pathetic but failed miserably, his eyes far too full of devilment to carry it off, and Maria couldn't help laughing.

'Well, in the face of such overwhelming logic how can I possibly refuse?' She tucked her hand in the crook of the elbow he offered, her fingers relishing the heat of his muscular arm through the fine cloth of his suit.

The warmth inside her owed little to the scant physical contact between them, being a direct result of the glow that she'd felt when he'd called her a beautiful woman. It might have been a throw-away line echoing what Hassan had said but it was something that she'd needed to hear—something every woman craves to hear from the man who has fathered her child.

Her footsteps faltered as the thought registered.

God! How could she have forgotten?

Her obstetrician had explored with her the possibility that her continued malaise during her pregnancy was due in part to the mental stress she was under. Maria had to admit that she thought he was right, her stomach tying itself in knots every time she remembered that at some stage she was going to have to tell Leo that she was carrying his child.

'Do you need to go home before we eat?' Leo's voice drew her back to the present and she was torn between running as far and as fast as she could to avoid the inevitable and getting the job over with.

'We might as well eat straight away,' she said decisively, raising her chin and squaring her shoulders as though preparing for battle. She'd never been brought up to be a coward and had no intention of starting now.

The restaurant that she directed him to was just around the corner from the hospital. She'd walked past it almost every day on her way to and from her flat and had heard from other members of staff that it was well worth a visit.

This evening, because of the unfashionably early hour, they were unlikely to encounter any colleagues who might have raised eyebrows at their apparent intimacy.

Of course, she thought as they were seated in a quiet corner in the nearly deserted room, it could be a positive boon to have the place empty if his reaction to her news was too violent.

A squadron of butterflies began formation-flying in her stomach as she tried to concentrate on making her selection from the menu.

'Need some help deciding?' Leo teased when the waiter returned to take their orders and she still hadn't chosen.

'I only want something fairly light,' she said faintly, worried that the morning sickness which had plagued her morning, noon and night might make a disastrous appearance if she had anything too rich.

'Would Madam like some melon for a starter and then perhaps chicken breasts poached in white wine sauce to follow?' The waiter's smile was nearly as wide as his waistline.

'That sounds wonderful,' Maria replied and managed to return his smile as the decision was made for her and she drew in a steadying breath while Leo ordered his own meal.

'So,' he turned his attention on her as soon as they were alone again. 'What made you decide to go into medicine? Is it a family thing?'

'I don't know,' she admitted openly, having long ago come to terms with the events of her childhood. 'I was fostered when I was seven by a wonderful couple called Anna and Luiz Martinez. Over the years they had a round dozen of us and the love they gave us just seemed to grow the more there were.' She couldn't help the warmth of the smile which took over her face at the happy memories.

'They must have been very proud of your achievement. It's a long haul to qualify as a doctor.'

'They always told us that the only thing they wanted was that we were the best we could be. Dustman or doctor didn't matter to them as long as we did the best we could.'

'Why the interest in haemoglobinopathies? Inherited disorders of haemoglobin structure aren't a particularly common specialisation.'

'Because my brother, Marco, had beta thalassaemia.'

'Had?' he questioned softly, his silvery eyes intent on hers across the candle-lit, linen-clad table.

She nodded. 'He died when he was eleven.'

'So, first you lost your parents and then your brother.' His soft voice spoke of sympathy but she couldn't allow the misapprehension to continue.

'We didn't lose our parents so much as they lost us,'
she said wryly. 'When Marco was born my father had
the son he always wanted. He was devastated when he
found out that his precious son had beta thalassaemia
and when it was confirmed that it was incurable he
made my mother dump the two of us in a hospital
waiting-room. Apparently they were on their way to
the airport on their way back to Italy for good.'

'Couldn't the authorities do anything?' He sounded
appalled.

'They did,' she smiled. 'They took us to Anna
and Luiz.'

'But what about your parents? They should have
taken responsibility for their own children,' he insisted.

'I think Marco and I had the best deal,' Maria said
confidently. 'Feeling the way they did, our parents
wouldn't have done nearly as good a job of raising us
and loving us as Anna and Luiz did.' She smiled as she
remembered her foster-parents' pleasure when she'd
asked to be allowed to adopt their surname.

'So, what happened to Marco? Was he particularly
badly affected by the disease?'

'I was too young at the time to realise the full extent
of what was going on but apparently our parents tried
for a long time to deny that there was anything wrong
with him. By the time he reached Anna's care his whole
system had been weakened by neglect, although I didn't
realise the implications of what I'd seen until I began
my medical training.' She looked off into the distance
as she called the details to mind.

'He was severely anaemic so he had no energy; his
spleen was massively enlarged so he had very little
appetite; his bone-marrow was hyperactive and this had

caused deformities to his skull and his long bones—virtually all the classic complications of untreated thalassaemia.'

She looked up at him and caught sight of that same haunted expression that she'd seen before.

'What about you?' she prompted before he had time to hide behind his self-protective barriers, intuition telling her that his pain went even deeper than her own. 'What made you specialise in this field?'

He was quiet for so long that Maria began to think that he wasn't going to answer.

'It's a similar story,' he said at last, his voice a low rasp as his eyes focused on the design he was tracing with the tines of his dessert fork. 'But, instead of a brother, I lost a son.'

'Oh, Leo,' she breathed, her heart going out to him in sympathy. 'Why? What happened?'

'There are so many similarities with Marco's story that it makes me feel ill,' he murmured in a deep rumble, the fork abandoned as he linked his fingers tightly together.

'No!' Maria was surprised into an instinctive denial. 'I don't believe you would ever abandon your child.' She reached out her hand and laid it over his tortured knuckles to reinforce her support but he drew his hands away and raised his eyes to meet hers.

'I might just as well have,' he said harshly. 'I was so busy being a doctor that I hardly had time to see him. He was just a little bundle asleep in bed.'

'What about your wife? Wasn't she there to look after him?'

'Just until he was six weeks old. Then she organised for someone to stay in the house with him so that she could go back to work. She told me she was only going back part-time but that was another of her lies. By the time I realised there was something wrong. . .' He shrugged helplessly.

'What about the blood tests? Why weren't they done?' Maria frowned. Something didn't seem quite right.

'They were but, as a haematologist, it was my dear wife who did them herself and didn't bother to tell me what she found.'

'But. . .'

'He had a stroke and died in my arms on his first birthday.' Leo's eyes were liquid with unshed tears as he gazed at her. 'I didn't know that I was a carrier of beta thalassaemia trait and Sophia had never bothered to tell me she was. Between us we doomed that little child to hell on earth. . .' His voice died away as his throat closed up and Maria felt her own eyes stinging in sympathy.

'Do you want to stay for dessert?' Maria murmured into the fraught silence. 'I can offer you some coffee back at my flat if you'd rather leave now.'

'Thanks.' He drew in a deep shuddering breath and nodded. 'I don't think either of us is in the right frame of mind to enjoy any more food. I'm only sorry I spoilt your meal.' He signalled to their waiter for the bill.

'You didn't spoil it.' She took a chance and covered his hand as it lay on the table, his tanned skin seeming even darker against the stark contrast of the white cloth. 'Sometimes the only time you can talk about the things that really matter is when you meet someone who's gone through similar experiences. I doubt if you've told anyone else what you've told me tonight.' She threw the words at him as a challenge and saw him blink then shake his head.

'You're quite right,' he admitted. 'My colleagues knew that my son had died but I couldn't bear to tell them any more than that. I just felt too guilty.'

He held her chair for her with innate good manners and they left the restaurant to find a thin cold rain falling.

'Let's go back in and call a taxi. It's miserable out here.' He leaned protectively over her to shelter her from the misty drizzle as he directed her back towards the door of the restaurant.

'It's not worth it,' she said impulsively. 'It's only a couple of minutes away. Let's walk.'

'Are you sure?' He turned towards her and carefully pulled the collar of her coat up around her ears to protect her from the weather, his hands coming to rest on her shoulders.

Maria nodded, glad that he wasn't able to read her mind as she admitted to herself that she was grasping at any opportunity to spend a little more time with him. Somehow she *had* to tell him her secret tonight. There was no knowing when she might have some time alone with him again.

She'd hoped that having a chance to talk to each other over a meal and learn a little about each other's lives would help her to find the perfect opportunity— would give her an idea how to go about it.

The only problem was that now she felt that she had even less idea how he'd react to her news.

All she could do was hope that, in spite of the shock, he would see that the child she was carrying could help to heal the scars of the past.

'Maria?' His voice was a low rumble in the quiet wetness of the deserted streets.

'Yes?' Tiny drops of water sparkled on her eyelashes as she angled her head to look up at him in the glow of the street-light, her arm tucked securely in the crook of his elbow as they made their way steadily through the darkness.

'Is there. . .?' He paused and she saw the droplets of rain in his dark hair strike pinpoints of diamond fire as he angled his head towards her. 'Are you seeing anyone from the hospital?'

She felt the tension in his body through her contact with his arm and wondered for one heart-stopping moment whether he had guessed why she had gone to see the obstetrician.

'Seeing anyone?' she repeated. 'What for?'

'A boyfriend, for want of a better word.' He pulled a face at the inappropriate phrase.

'Oh.' Relief that he hadn't guessed made her laugh breathlessly. 'No. As Hassan said, I don't really have time for much of a social life.'

'You must find it rather lonely—to go from the responsibility of the hospital to the quiet of your little home without anyone to talk to about what's happened during the day.'

She thought about it for a moment, playing his words over in her head and hearing his own loneliness behind them.

'I hadn't really thought of it like that before,' she admitted. 'I'm surrounded by so much hustle and bustle all day that the silence when I got home was like an oasis where I could recuperate.'

'And now?' he prompted.

'I suppose you're right about the lack of contact,' she said slowly. 'Sometimes it would be wonderful to unwind after a particularly gruelling shift by being able to talk to someone who understands what I'm talking about.'

'Would I do?'

His words hovered in the air in front of them and sheer surprise made Maria stumble over the edge of a paving slab.

Instantly Leo pulled his elbow to his side, trapping her arm against the warm security of his ribs to steady her.

'Do?' There was a quiver to her voice as she tried to keep her emotional responses under control in the face of his physical closeness and his apparent wish to be with her when she wasn't at work.

What exactly did he mean? Was he suggesting that the two of them should become 'an item', as the current phrase went, or did he just mean. . .?

'I could be the person you could talk to,' he clarified, then continued swiftly before she could answer almost as if he was afraid of hearing her reply. 'Now that I'm moving just a few miles down the road I'll be close enough to phone for a chat or for the two of us to go out for the occasional meal. We could act as a sort of safety valve for each other for when the pressure becomes unbearable.'

'A safety valve,' she repeated as her heart sank at the anti-climax. Why on earth had she leapt to the conclusion that he might be suggesting the start of a relationship between them?

'Well,' his voice sounded so calm and logical that she could have screamed, 'I know you aren't interested in a serious relationship at the moment—you're too wrapped up in your career. And I won't be making any commitments—not after my last disaster. Perhaps we could just start off with a sort of. . .friendship?'

What irony!

Maria was tempted to laugh out loud. Here she was walking arm in arm through the misty drizzle of a winter evening with the most attractive and interesting man she'd ever met and he was suggesting that they could develop some sort of friendship between them. The only trouble was that with her vivid memories of the most erotic night—the *only* erotic night—of her life there was little chance that she could ever see him as just a friend.

Still, she gave a swift sigh of regret, it was unlikely that his offer of friendship would survive the announcement that she intended to make before they parted company this evening so the whole question was all rather academic.

'No answer?' he prompted as he drew her to a halt outside her front door and she realised that her silence had stretched out too long.

'It's. . .difficult to know exactly what to say.' She found herself fumbling for words to convey her thoughts. 'After the way we met do you think it's feasible that we could start as if we'd only just met?'

He was silent for a moment, his eyes scanning her face as if he was trying to see her very thoughts and she found herself unable to look away, her own gaze locked on the planes and shadows of his enigmatic expression.

'I know what you mean,' he murmured at last, his voice sounding deeper in the hush as the rain finally stopped falling. 'I only have to hear your voice and I remember the sound of it the first time we met—your soft words in the darkness. I see you and my hands remember how unbelievably silky your skin felt against them and I want to take your clothes off to see if it feels as good as my memories tell me; to see what you look like in the light. . .'

'Leo. . .!' Suddenly her heart was in her throat, strangling any hope of speech as it beat out a frantic tattoo.

So, she wasn't the only one who remembered that night with pleasure; who remembered the soft words and softer caresses. . .

'Maria. . .' His voice was little more than a whisper as he drew her unresisting body towards him and circled her with his arms. 'I remember your kisses. . .' His lips were moving against hers as he spoke. 'After so long alone their softness brought me back to life with their sweetness and generosity.'

His palms cradled her chilled cheeks, his long fingers spearing the damp curly tendrils of hair as he tilted her face up for the full power of his kiss.

Maria melted against him, her arms circling his lean body when her legs refused to support her any longer and her hands unconsciously tracing the long muscular back she had first explored in all its naked glory so many weeks ago.

'Ah, sweetheart.' There was a trace of laughter in his voice as he tore his mouth away from hers and he captured her hands with his and she suddenly realised that she had feverishly begun to unfasten the buttons on his shirt.

When had she become so desperate to feel the supple heat of his body? She didn't know. All she did know was that she was standing on her front doorstep under the glare of a nearby street light in full view of any neighbour who happened to glance out of their window, trying to take Leo's clothes off.

'Oh, my God.' She drew her hands away as fast as if they'd touched a live wire. 'I'm sorry. . .I didn't mean. . .'

'I'm not,' Leo said firmly as he recaptured her hands and drew them back to his chest, holding them over his pounding heart with his own hands. 'The only thing I'm sorry about is that we have to stop long enough to get inside the front door.'

The increasing huskiness of his voice was proof enough that he meant every word but by the time she'd rummaged in the bottom of her bag for the key and turned it in the lock Maria had begun to regain control of her senses and turned to face him in the softly lit narrow hallway.

'Leo. . . We can't just. . .' Her words were lost in the renewed passion of his kiss as soon as the door closed behind them and Maria was overwhelmed by the heat of her response.

Never had she responded this fast or this wildly to *any* man but, with Leo, he only had to kiss her; only had to *look* at her to raise her temperature to flashpoint.

It was several moments before she realised that the heat she was feeling wasn't just due to her reaction to Leo's kiss. She'd been chilled by their leisurely walk in the drizzle and the sudden transition to the warmth of

her centrally heated flat was too much for the disturbed
equilibrium of her system.

'Leo,' she wailed distantly as everything slipped out
of focus and the world went black.

CHAPTER FOUR

MARIA swam slowly to the surface of a dark echoing well. In her ear was the deep rumble of indecipherable words, the tone one of worry as they gradually separated themselves out into speech.

'Maria? Sweetheart, what's the matter?' She felt the warmth of his hand on her forehead and his fingertips at her wrist as he checked her temperature and pulse.

The hint of a smile crept over her lips as she hazily took note of the care he was lavishing on her and then a frown pleated her forehead as she tried to work out what was going on.

'Leo?' She tried to lift her head but his hand cradled her cheek and persuaded her to lie back again.

'Stay still for a minute,' he ordered softly. 'You're still very white.' His fingers smoothed the wildly curly tendrils of hair away from her temple as she gazed up at him out of puzzled, dark honey eyes.

He must have carried her through from the hallway to lay her down on her bed—she knew that she had been in no fit condition to walk here herself. . .

'You're not taking proper care of yourself.' There was an undertone of anger in his voice but his expression was gentle as he finished unfastening her coat and helped her to slip her arms out of the sleeves. 'You shouldn't let yourself get to the stage where you pass out from exhaustion.'

'I think it was the heat,' she offered in a shaky voice,

remembering how hot the hallway had felt when she'd walked into the flat. 'It was too much of a contrast after the cold outside.'

'It's a lot warmer than this in the hospital and it didn't seem to affect you.' There was a frown pulling his dark brows together as he returned from draping her coat over the back of her chair and sat down on the side of the bed. 'And you were fine in the restaurant. . .'

He took possession of her wrist again, his keen grey eyes scanning her face as he noted the rapid tripping of her pulse, and Maria found herself unable to meet his gaze, afraid that he would be able to read her guilt over the secret she still had to tell him.

'What's going on, Maria?' He turned her back to face him with an unrelenting hand on her cheek, his eyes boring insistently into hers. 'What's the matter with you?'

She was peripherally aware that there was a strange note of fear in his voice, as if he thought that there might be something seriously wrong with her, but she dismissed the idea as fanciful as she finally found her tongue.

'Actually,' she began and had to clear the huskiness from her throat before she could continue—an awful premonition of disaster suddenly seizing her.

'Leo, there's something I should have told you. Something that happened. . .that's happening. . . It doesn't mean that I'll expect you to do anything. . .that I want you to be there when I. . .'

'Maria.' He was laughing at her incoherence as he captured the slender hands which were alternately wringing each other and waving agitatedly about.

'Slow down. I haven't the faintest idea what you're talking about.'

'Oh, Leo,' she subsided with a sigh and worried her lower lip between her teeth but there seemed to be no way to lead up to the subject, not when his silvery grey eyes were concentrating so hard on her. 'I'm pregnant,' she whispered at last.

She might as well have screamed the words at him for the effect they had.

'What!' His eyes darkened with a mixture of shock and dismay as he gazed rapidly from her face to her all-but-flat belly and back again, the shaking of his head signalling his disbelief as he began to fire questions at her faster than she could answer.

'When? I mean, how far. . .? *Who*?' This question was more insistent—almost an accusation. 'Who's the father? You said you weren't going out with anyone.'

'I wasn't. I'm not.' She felt terribly vulnerable, lying there under his angry gaze, but there was no way she could have found the energy to sit up; no way she *could* have with his broad shoulders looming over her that way. 'I'm four and a half months pregnant,' she said quietly and left him to draw his own conclusions.

'No. . .! Dear God, no!' His voice was filled with horror as he leapt up from the side of the bed to glare down at her and then began to pace furiously backwards and forwards across the width of the small room like a caged panther.

His instant rejection was so much more violent than anything she had imagined and her eyes filled with anguished tears as they followed him helplessly, each passage making the walls seem to crowd in closer together and the atmosphere grow more tense.

'Why didn't you tell me?' he demanded as he paused briefly at the foot of the bed, throwing the words at her like weapons before he continued on his agitated way. 'You knew about this months ago. You *must* have known last month when I came to find you and apologise. . .'

'*That* was the day I found out,' Maria interrupted bravely. 'It never occurred to me that the reason I wasn't feeling well was. . .'

'Why didn't you say something? I was here in your house—you should have told me then.' His glare was accusing as he stood over her, one clenched fist planted adamantly on each hip.

'Too much had happened that day.' Maria closed her eyes, unable to cope with the sight of his shirt stretched tautly across the broad chest she'd been exploring such a short while ago. She had to concentrate—to remember what had happened that other day or he'd never understand. . .

'I'd just had the shock of finding out I was pregnant by a man I'd never seen and had no means of finding when you turned up out of the blue. All that was on top of thirty-six hours of duty and covering for sick colleagues. I wasn't in a fit state to think straight,' she pleaded in the face of his closed expression. 'I needed time to sort out my. . .'

'Time!' he exploded. 'If you're already eighteen weeks pregnant time isn't a luxury we can afford!'

'W-what?' Maria frowned as she struggled to push herself up against her pillows, heartily sick of lying there like a stranded fish. 'What has time got to do with anything? I've still got another four and a half months before the baby's due. That should be plenty of time to make all the arrangements for. . .'

'You've got beta thalassaemia trait?' The sudden question sounded far more like an accusation and stopped her reassuring words instantly.

'Yes,' she confirmed. 'I probably mentioned that when I told you about Marco. . .'

'So have I,' he barked.

'I gathered that when you told me about your son's. . .'

'Have you been tested?' he demanded abruptly.

'I've had all my antenatal checks, if that's what you mean. I went along as soon as I was told I was. . .'

'No. I mean the chorionic villus sampling before you reached the tenth week,' he interrupted her again.

'I didn't even know I was pregnant until the twelfth week and, anyway, the CVS couldn't be done without a blood sample from both parents.'

'And you didn't know who I was.' He grimly nodded his understanding. 'What about foetal blood sampling? Have you had a percutaneous umbilical blood sample taken yet to find out whether the baby's positive?'

'No. . .'

'But you've arranged for it to be done in the next two weeks.' The words weren't intended as a question.

'No,' she repeated steadily.

'No? Why on earth not?' His growing anger was evident in the clenching and releasing of his fists, his eyes cold steel as they pierced her accusingly. 'You must realise how irresponsible that is. You know more about the curse of beta thalassaemia than most.'

'There's no point in being tested just for the sake of it,' she returned spiritedly, her chin coming up at the attack. She didn't like the way that he was constantly

interrupting her. 'For a start there's always a chance
that the test could cause a spontaneous abortion but. . .'

'What do you mean, ''just for the sake of it''?
There's a damn good reason for testing the baby and
you know it.' He looked as though he wanted to shake
her. 'We both carry the trait and, because of that, there's
a one-in-four chance that the baby has inherited the
disorder.'

'And a three-in-four chance that it hasn't but. . .'
she held up a shaky hand to prevent him breaking in,
determined that this time she would finish what she
wanted to say '. . .it doesn't matter either way because
I wouldn't even contemplate an abortion.'

Her fierce avowal silenced him but only momentarily.

'That's totally selfish and irresponsible,' he raged,
his face quite white in the subdued light of her bedroom
and his eyes dark coals just waiting to spit fire at her.
'Have you thought for a minute about the child's
rights—about *my* rights as the child's father?'

There was just time for Maria to register a pang that
the first time Leo mentioned his role as her baby's
father was in an argument over his right to decide
whether it would be allowed to live at all when her
staunch beliefs flooded in to support her.

'Of *course* I've thought about the baby—I've spent
the last month thinking about it constantly.' Suddenly
she was the epitome of a lioness defending her cub.
'As far as *your* rights are concerned—' she allowed
scorn to weight her tone '—not long ago you were at
great pains to tell me that you're not interested in any
permanent relationships. Well, that might be all right
for you—it sounds as if a one-night stand is about as

much as you can handle but whether it lives for a day or a full lifetime a baby is permanent.'

She saw the dark colour surge into his cheeks at her slighting reference to what had occurred between them but it hardly slowed the speed of his renewed attack.

'Have you thought about how you're going to cope if the baby *is* born with the disease?' he demanded, putting the ball straight back into her court.

'I'll probably cope just as well as any other mother will—probably marginally better. Considering the nature of my job, I know more than most about the physical and emotional needs of a child with beta thalassaemia.'

'Except you're not in the same position as any other mother, are you?' he accused coldly. 'You're not married so you won't have anyone there to help share the burden; to take their turn at sitting through a crisis so you can catch up on your sleep. If the way you collapsed this evening is any indication you aren't managing to take care of yourself properly *before* the baby arrives so how can you hope to do so afterwards?'

Maria gazed at him silently, holding all the hurt inside the way she'd learned to do so long ago when it had been her parents attacking her for her defence of her sickly little brother.

'So much for your offer of friendship,' she muttered under her breath as she rolled over and swung her feet to the floor. 'I can do without fair-weather friends.'

The sadness inside her heart was overwhelming but there was no way that she was going to let him know how much he'd wounded her.

She straightened up to her full height, swaying briefly as she got her balance rather than acknowledge the hand he reached out towards her.

'I think it's time you left,' she said quietly as she led the way towards the hall on shaky legs. 'I need to catch up on my sleep.' It was a petty dig at him but she wasn't feeling very noble at the moment.

'Maria. . .'

'No doubt we'll be bumping into each other at intervals.' She took great delight in cutting across his attempts at speech to deliver her final challenge. 'I shan't bother passing on any bulletins about the baby— unless you particularly want me to?'

She didn't know how she managed to keep her voice so calm and unemotional when all she wanted to do was scream and rail at the unfairness of it all.

It wasn't that she'd expected him to greet her sudden announcement with cries of joy—how could he when they barely knew each other and the whole situation had come about by accident? But she hadn't anticipated his demand that she have the baby tested to see whether he wanted it to be aborted, nor the attack on her capabilities as a mother.

She felt very small and alone as she stood in the hallway holding the front door open for him, shivering as the chilly wind whipped her clothes around her and teased out the newly dried strands of hair while she stared stonily out into the night.

'For God's sake, woman. We've got to talk about this. Throwing me out doesn't solve anything.' His frustrated voice came from a point right behind her shoulder but she refused to turn and face him, not certain how well she would be able to hide her feelings from him if he didn't leave soon.

'Neither does ranting at me,' she said softly as

she tightened her chilly fingers around the catch. 'Especially when I won't be changing my mind.'

'Well, neither will I,' his voice grated over her raw nerves, his words a heartbreaking mixture of determination, frustration and despair. 'Dammit, I've already been through this once. I couldn't bear to see it all happen a second time.'

Maria watched silently as he stepped past her and out of her flat, turning his shoulders so that there was no chance of any contact between them. She waited for him to turn back; waited for some sort of farewell before he left but he strode away from her, his shoulders hunched defensively inside his jacket as he disappeared into the shadows of the night.

'Dr Martinez?' the young nurse hailed her just as she was making her way out of the ward and Maria sighed tiredly.

'Yes, Nurse?' She waited by the door, unwilling to walk any further than she had to on her aching feet.

'There's been a message up from Emergency. Shabana Saleh is on her way up.'

Maria nodded, her shoulders slumping in spite of her best efforts as she realised that there was now no chance of getting home early. Shabana was one of her 'special' children and the only reason she would be coming in like this when she wasn't due for a transfusion was that she was having a sickle cell crisis.

'Oh, Doctor, I'm so glad you're here.' Mrs Saleh managed a small smile but most of her attention was on her little daughter.

'How is she?' Maria asked while she began her

examination. 'Have you any idea what brought the crisis on this time?'

'It's all my fault,' the poor woman wailed softly as she comforted the little girl on her lap. 'But all her new friends at school had been invited to the party, too, and I hated to have to say no.'

'What sort of party was it, Shabana?' Maria questioned while she noted the six-year-old's paleness in spite of her raised temperature.

'A birthday party for Amy,' she whispered weakly. 'We went to the swimming pool.' She paused to wince as Maria examined her painful joints and then continued gamely. 'Then, afterwards, we had cake with candles.'

'In the swimming pool?' Maria demanded in careful mock amazement. 'How did you get the candles to stay alight?'

'Not in the water!' She pulled a face at Maria's silliness. 'Afterwards. When we finished swimming.'

'Did you all get dressed up in party dresses to have your cake?' she prompted.

'No. We had our swimming costumes on.' Her eyes closed as she rested her head against her mother's shoulder, a small grey rabbit clutched tightly in the crook of one arm.

'So,' she murmured to the worried parent. 'It was a case of too much strenuous exercise and excitement, followed by standing around and getting chilled.'

'Yes, Doctor. If only I'd realised that they weren't going to get dressed straight away. . . She never has this problem after her swimming lessons because the teachers make sure she doesn't stand around. They send her off to change straight away then go to her next lesson.'

Maria saw the woman's eyes stray to a point just behind her but she had no need to look to see who was there. Even if she hadn't recognised the individual mixture of soap and musky male which had been imprinted on her memory for ever one dark passionate night the tiny hairs on the back of her neck had lifted at his proximity in spite of her determination not to respond.

'Well, Mrs Saleh, we'll get Shabana on a drip straight away to dilute her blood and we'll give her something to take the pain away. If I could get you to make sure that she drinks plenty of fluids?'

'What would be best to give her?' The poor mother was only too willing to help.

'Whatever she wants—fruit juice, water, milk—the same as you would give her at home. Just ask the nurses and they'll get whatever she prefers to make sure she'll drink plenty to get her levels up.'

'Have you found anything in particular that helps your daughter to cope with the pain?' Leo's deep voice joined in the discussion. 'Some children prefer to lie still with the painful areas supported on soft pillows; others need to be distracted by someone reading to them or watching a favourite film.'

'Shabana likes me to rock her and sing to her.' Maria watched, unsurprised as Mrs Saleh responded shyly to Leo's charisma. 'She just likes to curl up on my lap with her rabbit and wait for the pain to go away while she listens.'

'She's a lucky girl to have a mother who can sing her pain away,' he said with a gentle smile for the two of them and Maria's heart ached at the evidence of a gentler side to his nature.

It was another half-hour before Maria felt happy about leaving the ward but Peg Mulholland had come on duty and she trusted her to know when to call for assistance if Shabana didn't respond as anticipated.

She half expected to find Leo waiting for her outside in the corridor but it was nearly as deserted as the rest of the hospital corridors at this time of day as she walked towards the main entrance and out into the dark evening.

As she made her weary way home she tried to remember what she'd been doing during the day to make her feel so exhausted but couldn't pinpoint anything out of the ordinary. As far as she could see there were only two major differences in her life these days—her slowly progressing pregnancy and her lack of sleep—either one of which could be responsible for the fact that she just wanted to curl up on the nearest flat surface and sleep for a week.

Unfortunately, as soon as she closed her eyes she was plagued with thoughts of Leo da Cruz; with memories of the incredible pleasure he'd brought her interspersed with his fury at her refusal to consider that the baby they'd created might not be worth carrying. . .

'What the hell do you think you're doing, woman?' an angry voice sounded in her ear as she turned towards her front door and she uttered a strangled shriek as she nearly leapt out of her skin.

'Leo!' she breathed as her pulse thundered in her ears. 'You startled me. What are you. . .?'

'You shouldn't be wandering about the streets on your own at this time of night. Haven't you got the sense God gave a goose? Where's your car?'

'What car?' she snapped back, her sudden surge of pleasure at seeing him totally destroyed by his auto-cratic attitude. 'I only live a few hundred yards from the hospital. What on earth would I need a car for?'

'But. . .what do you do when it's raining?' He sounded nonplussed by her logic.

'I'm not made of sugar—I don't dissolve,' she pointed out sarcastically. 'And walking's good for the baby.'

She turned away from his steely gaze and concen-trated on getting her key out, pausing directly in front of him until he stepped aside for her to reach the lock.

'Has your purpose in coming here been satisfied by shouting at me or do you want to say something more?' She threw the barbed question over her shoulder as she entered the hallway.

'Of course I want to say something more,' he ground out through gritted teeth. 'I told you last time that we needed to talk. . .'

'And *I* told you there was nothing to talk about,' she reminded him as she walked calmly towards the kitchen, leaving him to close the front door for her.

He must have paused in the hallway to regain control of his temper because the kettle was almost boiling by the time he arrived in the doorway.

'Tea or coffee?' Maria offered without looking up from the mugs she was setting on the tray.

'I haven't come here for a teaparty,' he said in a voice that was a chilling mixture of ice and gravel. 'I came to talk some sense into you.'

'Well.' She threw a bland smile at him as she opened a packet of biscuits and fanned them into an expert semicircle on a matching plate. 'I'm sure you'll feel far better if you get something warm inside you first. You must have got quite chilled waiting for me on the doorstep.' She poured water onto instant decaffeinated coffee granules in each of two mugs. 'Milk and sugar?' she demanded brightly.

'For God's sake!' he exploded, throwing both hands theatrically up in the air in one of the first really 'foreign' displays Maria had seen from him. She smiled as it drew to mind fond memories her of her foster-father in one of his volcanic Italian tantrums—the sort that his wife had been able to defuse with nothing more than a kiss even when she was the cause of it.

For all that Leo had told her that he was half Italian and half Greek until now the only evidence she had seen of it was his Mediterranean colouring and his charm. She found it fascinating to discover this whole new facet of his personality.

'I'm glad you find the situation so amusing,' he snapped as he reached for the tray. 'I presume you want this taken into the lounge?' He turned and marched out, leaving Maria hovering over the milk jug and sugar bowl.

'Blow it,' she muttered. 'He can just have his black,' and she followed him through to the other room.

He'd made himself comfortable at one end of the settee, the tray on the table he'd pulled in front of it. When she collected her mug and settled herself in her usual chair on the other side of the room he scowled blackly but refrained from making any comment, even when he tasted his coffee and pulled a face.

The silence between them took on a life of its own, growing denser and more menacing the longer it went on. Finally Maria couldn't bear it any longer and took the initiative.

'You said you wanted to speak to me?' she prompted as she curled her feet up under her on the seat. For the first time she was aware that it wasn't quite as easy to fold herself up so small and she realised that after months of being a secret presence inside her the baby was finally making his or her presence felt.

Her heart gave a little lift as she realised that any day now she would be able to feel real signs of move-ment—not just the faint flutters she'd been aware of for the last few weeks.

'What. . .?' She suddenly realised that Leo had been speaking and in her preoccupation with the develop-ment of the baby she'd completely missed it.

'I said,' he repeated drily, 'have you thought any more about what I said?'

'What in particular?' Maria enquired, refusing to rely on any guesswork. This whole situation was far too important to disintegrate in misunderstandings.

'About having the baby's blood tested,' he said, his voice sharp with tension.

'No.'

'But. . .'

'Leo,' she broke in firmly before he could get in his stride, 'I will *not* be having the baby tested for beta thalassaemia before it's born. That is my choice and it's my *right* to make that choice.'

'And what about *my* rights?' he countered. 'What if I go to court to make you have the test?'

'You could try—and you might even be able to persuade a judge that the tests are a good idea.'

She wrapped both hands round the mug of rapidly

cooling coffee to steady her shaking fingers as she watched the surprised expression cross his face.

'Of course I would oppose the idea on several grounds, the first being that the test could provoke premature labour.'

'You know as well as I do how rare that is these days.' There was open disgust in his voice.

'But do the solicitors and judges? Would they want to be responsible for forcing me to have a non-essential medical procedure which precipitated the death of my baby?'

'It wouldn't take long to produce the statistics to prove my case—both for testing the baby's blood and for the safety of the technique.'

'It might not take long but would it take too long?' she threw the words back at him. 'Every day that it takes to persuade a judge to see your point of view is a day closer to the legal deadline.

'Then,' she continued inexorably, 'when you add in the length of time it takes to do the necessary tests on the blood sample you've still got to go back to court if it turns out to be positive and persuade the judge that it's your right to kill the baby that I'm carrying inside my body.'

She was trembling all over by the time she finished, her knuckles gleaming white under the central light as they clenched tightly around her mug.

'You make a pretty good case, based on emotions,' he admitted bleakly. 'But, luckily, the law doesn't care about that. It's more concerned with justice and legal rights.'

He stood up suddenly, as though he couldn't bear to sit still any more, his long legs eating up the space backwards and forwards between her furniture.

'Oh, don't think I couldn't put forward an emotional argument just as heart-wrenching as yours,' he said bitterly. 'Apart from my professional evidence I could tell them at first hand what it's like to watch your son die of the complications associated with beta thalassaemia; of the agony and frustration of watching his pain and holding him in my arms as he died.'

'But that isn't a fair comparison with what would happen to this child,' she objected furiously as she protectively cradled the slight bump below her waist with one palm. 'He didn't receive the treatment he should have had. . .'

Like a cornered panther, he turned on her with a snarl.

'And can you give me a guarantee that the baby won't have a stroke or a heart attack or its lungs won't collapse? By what right do you decide unilaterally that you will put an unborn innocent through that? Half of his genetic inheritance comes from my genes and that means I have the right to share in making the decisions that concern him.'

'What right?' she demanded very softly, knowing that her next argument would make him more angry than ever. 'If I cast doubt on the possibility that you're the father of the baby you can't prove it without testing the baby's DNA.

'*That*,' she stressed, 'will take you back even further than where you started because unless you can prove you are the baby's father you have no right to demand *anything* and if I deny it you'll have to wait until the baby's born before I agree to the DNA testing.'

He stared at her in silence, his face nearly grey with shock that she would go so far.

'That would be professional suicide for you,' he whispered in horror, obviously realising for the first time just how determined she was. 'The publicity the case would collect would guarantee that the newspapers would drag your name through the mud.'

' "Promiscuous paediatrician",' Maria mimicked a tabloid headline. ' "Respectable lady doctor in a series of one-night stands. Doesn't know who her baby's father is." '

'It's not a bloody joke,' he snapped furiously.

'Matters of life and death rarely are,' she said soberly and sighed. 'So, where does that leave us?'

'God only knows.' He ran his fingers through his hair and cradled the back of his neck as though it ached. 'Who would have thought that a few minutes of forgetfulness could cause such upheaval?'

Maria snorted. 'I wonder how many people have said the same thing when they discover an unexpected pregnancy?'

Leo's attempt at a smile was more like a wry grimace but it was evidence that he was beginning to calm down a little.

'Look. . .' he paused to extract his wallet and take out a small white card '. . .this is the number for an answering service. If you need to get hold of me they'll know where I can be contacted.' He started to hold it out towards her then changed his mind and put it down on the table beside his empty coffee-mug as though he didn't want to get any closer to her.

'Where will you be?' Her voice was strangely husky as she looked up at him and contemplated the very real possibility that this might be the last time that she would see him in anything other than a professional context.

'I need to do some thinking,' he said sombrely, his hands pushed deep into his trouser pockets as he contemplated the muted pattern on the carpet. 'I've got about a month to go on my present contract; then I was going to do a couple more lectures before I took a holiday. You can expect to see me back at St Augustine's in about six weeks—if you don't hear from me in the meantime.'

He paused briefly on his way out of the room and looked back at her as she sat in her chair, stunned by the speed of events. Her eyes travelled greedily over him, trying to store his image as clearly as possible so that she could recall it over the next six weeks, and then he was gone.

CHAPTER FIVE

'CHAOS,' panted Peg Mulholland as she helped one of the more junior nurses moving the ward furniture around.

'All in a good cause, though,' Maria reminded her. 'It will mean that Katy and Laura Johnson can be in adjacent beds.'

Peg's expression softened. 'Poor kids,' she murmured, making sure that only Maria could hear her. 'One of them in for leg-lengthening and the other has her leg broken in an accident on her way here to visit her. No wonder they're desperate to stay close to each other.'

Maria had spent a frustrating afternoon trying to sort the problem out.

After the ward round to review the children hoping to go home she'd spent a long time between the computer and the telephone trying both to empty beds and to move children around to enable the Johnson sisters to share one side of the little four-bedded ward.

It had been just one more task at the end of a crippling day, the fact that it had been her turn to be on call today meaning that she'd been up and down between the ward and the accident department answering bleeps more times than she could remember.

It hadn't helped that the closest bank of lifts to the paediatric ward was undergoing major safety repairs.

After the first circuitous journey around the rabbit

warren of corridors and down to the ground floor she'd decided that it was faster to use the stairs than take the long way round to the next set of lifts. It was only now, hours later, that she was realising just how exhausting it was to spend so much time running up and down stairs.

The one thing that was keeping her going was the hope that Leo would contact her soon.

Each morning she woke up with the conviction that today was the day that she'd look up from tending a patient or reassuring worried parents and there he'd be, smiling his heart-stopping smile just for her.

Unfortunately it hadn't happened yet and, as a result, she still wasn't managing to get a good night's sleep and the drain on her system was beginning to tell.

Then, last night, she'd ended up staying on so late at the hospital with one of her 'special' children that it wasn't worth going home at all. She'd only got through by snatching a couple of hours' sleep on the narrow bed in the on-call room before it was time to start another day.

Meals were another problem which weren't helping her situation, with her erratic visits to the cafeteria or the staff canteen sometimes forgotten altogether. Even when she did manage to get her food on time there was no guarantee that she wasn't going to lose it all in another episode of lingering morning sickness.

'You're not looking so good,' Peg commented in her usual outspoken way as Maria made her shaky way into her office after her latest bout of nausea had robbed her of her tea. 'If you don't put on a bit more weight we'll have to start nailing your feet to the floor or you'll blow away in the breeze.'

'Jealousy gets you nowhere,' Maria teased, knowing

the ward sister was fighting a permanent battle with her weight.

'Seriously, though,' Peg insisted after she'd stuck an impudent tongue out at her. 'Have you been for a check-up? You look as if you could do with some vitamins or something.'

'If the "or something" is an all-expenses-paid trip to somewhere warm with nothing to do but laze around in the sun I might take you up on the prescription.' Maria smiled then pulled a wry face as her pager bleeped yet again. 'If you want to know why I don't put on any weight blame this thing.' She waved the offending electronic gadget aloft as she reached for the telephone.

'Another trip downstairs,' she sighed. 'Child without a seat belt in a multiple car shunt. See you later.'

She let herself out of the ward and set off along the corridor at a fast clip, the journey towards the echoing stairwell second nature to her by now.

'Jeremy? Can you hear me, love? Can you give my fingers a squeeze?' Maria smiled her relief as she felt the distinct increase in pressure. 'Good boy,' she praised as she went on with her examination, detailing one of the casualty staff to warn the appropriate department that Jeremy would shortly be coming up for a scan.

'Do we know who's on duty in Neurosurgery?' she demanded as she checked the child's pupil dilation again, her mouth pursing with worry. 'Depending on the results of the scan, this young man might have to pay him a rapid visit.'

'Do you want to have a quick word with the parents?'

Staff Nurse looked at her hopefully. 'I put them in the little interview room.'

'There's not much I can tell them yet but I'll give them what I've got,' Maria agreed, waiting until Jeremy was on his way for the scan before she went out to find them.

'Mr and Mrs Tolliver? I'm Dr Martinez.' She shook hands with each of them, knowing how important that brief physical contact could be to terrified parents. 'I've just examined Jeremy but he needs to have some tests done before I can be sure whether there's any damage.'

It took some time to calm the pair of them down, their guilt at not insisting that their spoilt only son stayed strapped in his seat belt making them alternately aggressive and apologetic.

By the time she'd managed to track the neurosurgeon down for an opinion on the brain scan and checked to see that Jeremy had been settled safely into ICU she had begun to feel quite strange, her head almost feeling as if it was floating several inches above her body as she made her way, yet again, up the stairs.

She'd nearly reached the top when her pager went off, the bleep startling her as it echoed eerily off the bare walls so that she almost missed her step.

In slow motion she watched her hand reach out for the hand-rail and grasp it and felt her feet tread almost silently from one step to the next until she got as far as the landing.

By concentrating all her energy she succeeded in touching the doorhandle leading to the corridor beside the lifts and even managed to pull it open part-way and step into the opening.

The last thing she remembered going through her

bewildered mind was that there was a black hole opening up at her feet. Suddenly she was convinced that
somehow she had managed to open the wrong door—
that, instead of walking out into the corridor, she had
stepped into the lift before the men had finished the
repairs and she was about to fall to the bottom of the
empty shaft.

'Maria. . .?'

She knew that she must be dreaming because that
was Leo's voice and these days he only ever spoke to
her in her dreams. She squeezed her lids tightly shut,
knowing that if she allowed herself to wake up properly
it would be the start of just another day without him.

'Come on, Maria. Open your eyes.'

This time she felt gentle fingers smoothing the
unruly tendrils of hair away from her face and she
breathed in the indefinable mixture of soap and man
that was Leo's alone.

'Leo?' she croaked as she looked up at him.
'What. . .what are you doing here?'

She couldn't see his expression—his head was outlined against a bright light as he leaned over her and
gazed into her eyes with professional detachment.

'I'm checking you over, you stupid woman,' he muttered under his breath out of deference to the nurse
hovering just behind him.

'What are you checking me over for? I'm perfectly
all right.' She glared indignantly up at him, feeling like
an upturned beetle under a microscope.

'Ha! So perfect that you passed out in the corridor,'
he scoffed.

'That's. . .that's only because I ran up the stairs from

the accident department. I. . .I must have taken it
too fast.'

'For God's sake, woman. Why didn't you take the
lift? It's not as if you need the exercise.' She could
almost feel the lightning glance over her body. 'You're
nothing but skin and bones.'

'I would have taken the lift if it was working,' she
returned with an air of long suffering. 'As it is it takes
longer to go around to the next bank of lifts than to go
down the stairs.'

'Couldn't you have sent one of the nurses instead?'

'Hardly. I'm on call today.'

'On call? You mean you've been dashing up and
down those stairs all day?' He sounded appalled.

'It feels as if I've been doing it for a month,' she
admitted wryly. 'Thank God, tomorrow's my easy
day—consultant ward round in the morning and diabetic clinic in the afternoon.'

'That's if you're fit enough to come in at all,' he
said grimly.

'What do you mean?' She batted away the hand
resting on her shoulder so that she could roll herself
over and sit up. 'Of course I'll be here—I'm on duty.'

'We'll see about that.' He nodded to the silent nurse
that she wasn't needed any more and she left the room,
her reluctance to leave the fascinating discussion evident as she looked back over her shoulder.

'For goodness' sake,' Maria hissed as she watched
the door swing closed on her avid face. 'The whole
hospital will be talking if you carry on like an over-
protective husband. What are you doing here, anyway?'

'Taking care of you as you don't seem to be doing
a very good job of it yourself.' He paused to steady

her as she slid off the high bed and fumbled her feet into her shoes. 'If you tell me where to find your bag you can wait here while I fetch it and then I'll take you home.'

'You certainly will not!' Maria glanced at her watch. 'I've still got several hours of work to do before I go off duty. In case you've forgotten I'm on call today.'

'That's all taken care of,' he said firmly. 'Now, just tell me where your. . .'

'What do you mean, it's "all taken care of"? What have you done?' There was an awful sinking feeling in her stomach. So far only her obstetrician knew about the baby. Had he unwittingly broadcast the reason why her health seemed to be so precarious at the moment. . .?

'I spoke to the registrar—Ian Stanton? He said he was only too willing to take over for you—said he owed you for several favours you've never let him repay.'

'But. . .'

'No more.' He held up both palms to stop her arguments. 'I'm going to be taking you home as soon as we collect your belongings and you're going to smile and say, "Thank you, Leo," with your best party manners.'

Maria subsided with a heavy sigh. As she ungraciously told him where her coat and bag were she resigned herself to being the object of the latest round of gossip and speculation. As long as the hospital grapevine never got to hear about what had happened in Italy she would be able to ride it out but if *that* ever became public knowledge. . .

She cringed at the thought, only then wondering

whether Leo was going to insist that she go all the way around to the next bank of lifts and if he would try to force her into the indignity of using a wheelchair.

As is the way with such things by the time she was ready to leave the department the repairmen had finished their job and the lift was back in full operation, whisking them swiftly and silently to the ground floor.

Once outside, instead of the waiting taxi she expected, he led her towards the consultants' car park, stopping beside a gleaming white BMW.

'Whose is this?' She gazed admiringly at the powerful lines of the car, thinking how well it suited him. 'Is someone lending you their car to take me home?'

'It's mine.' He opened the passenger door for her and waited until she was settled before he closed it again and went round to get behind the wheel. 'You wouldn't have seen it before because it was being serviced last time I came down.'

He secured his seat belt and flicked a glance across at hers before he switched on the engine and pulled out.

'Maria, I. . .'

'Leo, you. . .'

They began simultaneously then broke off and laughed.

'Ladies first,' he offered, concentrating on the traffic as he turned towards Alma Road.

'You said you weren't coming back for six weeks. . .' She allowed the words to die away, hoping that he would take it as a hint to explain why he had come so much sooner.

'I wasn't going to but when I heard that you'd collapsed I came straight. . .'

'Just a minute,' she interrupted indignantly. 'What

do you mean? *How* did you find out?'

He pulled a wry face, like a young boy caught out in a mischievous prank, but her blood began to boil and she pressed for an answer.

'You haven't been near the hospital for weeks so how have you been keeping tabs on me? How could you possibly know I'd been taken ill?' A sudden thought struck her. 'You've set someone to spy on me!' she cried, horrified at the very idea.

'I asked someone to let me know how you were in case you needed me,' he said stiffly, colour darkening his cheek-bones. 'I wasn't certain that you would call me yourself.' He drew the car up outside her house and leant forward to turn off the engine.

'You needn't bother doing that,' Maria sniped. 'I'll get out and you can be on your way.' She released her seat belt and swung the door open but he was there before her, his hand outstretched to assist her out of the contoured seat.

'I can manage,' she snapped, motioning his hand away.

'I'm sure you can but why not take advantage of the help when it's there?' He grasped her elbow and steadied her with an encircling arm when she found that her legs were still unsteady.

Her half-formed plan to be inside her flat before he'd finished locking the car came to nothing when he pointed a little gadget and the locks clicked simultaneously.

'Go through and put your feet up while I put the kettle on,' he ordered when he'd closed the door behind himself and turned towards the kitchen, for all the world as if *he* was the host. 'Decaffeinated coffee or tea?'

'Please, *do* make yourself at home!' Maria muttered sarcastically as she slid her feet gratefully out of her shoes and padded towards her favourite chair.

If she was honest it was wonderful to have someone there to make her a drink while she waited for her batteries to recharge. It was a novelty that she could grow quite accustomed to. . .

'Maria?'

'Oh.' She'd completely forgotten to answer. 'Tea, please. Not too strong and no sugar.'

'Are you sure you don't want some sugar to boost your energy?' His head appeared around the corner, one eyebrow raised questioningly.

'Not if you want me to be able to drink it. I can't stand sweet tea.' She shuddered at the thought. 'There's a packet of chocolate biscuits behind the. . .'

'Found them,' he interrupted.

'*How* did you find them? They were hidden away so I'd have something in case of visitors.'

'I think it's a system rather like radar,' he called back, his voice coming closer as he brought the tray through. 'Only in my case it works on chocolate biscuits!' The accompanying grin was infectious and Maria had a glimpse of how he must have been as a boy.

With a sudden leap she wondered if their child—the boy or girl she was nurturing inside her as they spoke—had inherited that grin. She found herself hoping fervently that they had, in spite of the fact that it would make it very hard to forget Leo once he had gone out of their lives.

'How's the tea?' his deep voice floated into her thoughts and she glanced down at the half-empty cup in her hand, suddenly aware that her mental meanderings hadn't prevented her from accepting the tea and beginning to drink it. 'Perfect.' She smiled distractedly, her mind still half-occupied with thoughts of the uncertain future.

'Maria?'

Once again she was called back to the present by his deep voice and this time she made an effort to pay attention.

'I'm sorry. I was wool-gathering.'

'Are you feeling any better?' There was honest concern in his voice. 'Peg Mulholland said you were unconscious for a good half-hour.'

'Probably the best sleep I've had in a long time.' She pulled a wry face. 'But I still don't understand how you got there so fast. You must have been sitting in your car just waiting for something to happen.'

'Not quite.' He laughed, his teeth gleaming whitely against the permanent tan of his Mediterranean ancestry. 'I had decided to pay a visit to the hospital and was just about to leave when the phone rang.'

'And who is your mole? Is it someone I know?' She had calmed down enough to smile at the cloak-and-dagger feel to the situation.

'Yes, but I promised I wouldn't be the one to tell you. They want a chance to tell themselves—if you'll excuse the scrambled grammar—I don't want to give away the person's gender.'

Suddenly she was secretly glad that whoever it was had contacted Leo. Now that she'd had time to think about it it had been a wonderfully comforting feeling to be taken care of and cosseted this way.

'Leo?' She spoke before she could get cold feet.

'Thank you for coming. It's nice to know that someone cared.'

'I think you'd be surprised exactly how many people care about you,' he said seriously. 'Not just your "special" kids and their families but everyone on the ward, too. They're worried about you.'

'Worried? But why?'

'Because they can see there's something wrong with you and don't know what to do or what to say.'

'And I don't know how I'm going to tell them.' She busied herself putting her empty cup down on the table and then reached out to switch on the corner lamp. The evening had become quite dark while they were sitting talking.

'I think the bigger problem is going to be *when* you tell them,' he suggested.

'Why? The pregnancy's hardly showing yet and I've still got several months before I start my maternity leave.'

'If you carry on the way you're going it'll be much sooner than that,' he warned seriously.

'But I can't afford to leave any sooner. There are all those patients who. . .'

'Unless you don't care about the baby's health?'

The open challenge in his words made her subside instantly.

'Of course I care about the baby,' she said softly, gazing at him steadily across the room. 'I wouldn't have dared to stand up to your bullying last month if I hadn't cared.'

They were both silent for a moment, remembering the confrontation, before she continued in a worried tone.

'But, Leo, I don't want to have to leave work early. I'd probably go mad with boredom if I just had to sit here for several months waiting for the baby to arrive— apart from the fact that the hospital won't have had a chance to find a replacement for me. And it wouldn't be fair to my colleagues or the patients if I leave them without adequate notice.'

'Can I offer a suggestion?' He was watching her closely as if trying to judge how she would take his words. 'I could take some of the pressure off you by arranging a temporary job-share. I'm sure the hospital management won't mind as long as they're getting the same number of hours' work for the same pay.'

'It couldn't possibly work,' Maria objected, after taking a startled moment to think about it. 'You'd end up killing yourself if you had to drive all those miles backwards and forwards day after day. It's a wonderful idea but it just wouldn't be practical with you living so far away.'

'It's a little over ten miles,' he said quietly.

'Ten. . .? But. . .' Her brows drew together in confusion as she tried to remember exactly how far away the Waverley hospital was.

'I moved into a place of my own last week from the staff flat. It just happens to be on this side of the Waverley.'

She pinpointed the area in her head. 'So you're actually living between the two hospitals,' she confirmed.

'That's right. And the roads are quite straightforward so, logistically, it could work, especially as I've also got some holiday time coming up.'

'But what would we say to St Augustine's? What reason could we give?'

'I take it you still haven't told anyone yet?'

She looked down at her fingers and found herself twining them together in her lap, unable to meet the laser intensity of his eyes as she shook her head. 'I don't know how,' she whispered. 'I know it happens all the time these days and people hardly take any notice but. . .' She drew in a shuddering sigh.

'But Anna and Luiz didn't raise you that way.' He supplied the missing words then he, too, fell silent.

Maria was beginning to feel uncomfortable under the fierceness of his gaze when he abruptly straightened out of the corner of the settee and began to pace.

As she watched him travel backwards and forwards she smiled inwardly. She'd watched him doing this before and recognised his action as evidence of stress.

Suddenly he stopped in front of her, leaning forward to place one hand on each arm of the chair as he fixed her eyes with his.

'We could get married,' he said without warning and her heart leapt into her mouth as she gazed up at him so close in front of her, a strange warmth spreading inside her at the thought of marriage to Leo.

'It would protect your reputation from the gossips,' he continued persuasively, unaware that those extra words were the icy blast that killed the little blossom of hope she hadn't been aware of nurturing along with the baby deep inside her.

'You can't get married just to stop gossip. Marriage is too precious to treat it like a coat of whitewash.' Her voice was harsh in her sudden disappointment and, even as she spoke, she realised how stupid she was being. There had never been any question of a permanent relationship between them so why should she be feeling cheated that he was making a suggestion based on logic?

'It would also give the baby a name so it wouldn't be born illegitimate,' he pointed out soberly, straightening away from her to resume his pacing.

'But. . .' Her thoughts were whirling. 'You don't *want* to get married. You said you wouldn't go through it again. . .*and* you don't want to have anything to do with the baby.'

He was on the other side of the room when he stopped pacing and stared across at her as if he was seeing her for the first time. A whole range of emotions crossed his face as she watched, the mixture far too complex for her to decipher.

'The situation has changed,' he said at last, his voice strangely rough. 'Whatever the rights and wrongs of how we arrived at this point, you're carrying my baby and it's up to me to take care of you.'

In his words Maria heard the echo of his insistence that it had been her parents' responsibility to stay to take care of Marco and herself and she felt another fragment of her dreams shatter. Once she'd longed to be a part of a real family—a family that loved each other and cared for each other because of that love.

Leo's offer, generous though it was, didn't have the same ring to it.

'I need to think about this,' she said into the stillness of the room and watched his shoulders stiffen, his face becoming expressionless as if he'd just put shutters up to stop her looking in.

'Maria, you. . .'

'Please, Leo,' she silenced him. 'Too much has happened today for me to think clearly. This has come at me out of the blue and I don't want to say anything for a few days. *You* might go home and realise that there are other, less drastic, solutions to the problem.'

'All right,' he agreed. 'If you think we need a short cooling-off period I'll back off but, while you're doing your thinking, don't forget that the baby needs a healthy mother and not one who's permanently exhausted. Whatever you decide the present situation can't go on for much longer.'

He'd left soon after, apparently unable to relax with so much unspoken tension between them. His final words before he let himself out of the front door were an order to get herself into bed as soon as possible to catch up on some of the sleep she needed.

'As if I'm going to be able to go straight to sleep after he delivers a bombshell like that!' she complained aloud as she tried to relax in a deep soothing bath filled with her favourite bubbles. 'Right out of the blue without a single word of warning. ''We could get married,'' he says, as calmly as if he was offering me another cup of tea.'

The indignation had long gone by the time she was curled up in bed and she rested her hand over the gentle curve of her belly.

'What should I do, little person? I don't know what's the best course. If we *have* given you beta thalassaemia between us, would it be better for you to have two parents to help to take care of you, even though one of them is only going to be there out of a sense of duty? Or would it be better if it was just the two of us—our own little loving family?'

She heard the echo of her wistful words and it reminded her of all her long-ago dreams.

Oh, she and her brother had started off with all the right ingredients for the perfect family but how quickly that had fallen apart. Then, such a short time later, she'd lost Marco, too, and it was only Anna's and Luiz's care that had helped her to survive.

The trouble was that she'd had to share them with so many others and, for all their loving attention, they hadn't been her own family.

She pulled a face in the dark as she realised that since Anna and Luiz had died she'd all but lost contact with the other members of their 'family'—but somehow it was hard to feel guilty. They'd been brought up to be strong and independent so it was hardly surprising that they had all gone their separate ways.

Now she was expecting a baby of her own—the start of her very own family—but the joy was tempered by the gap in the circle where a loving husband should be.

Leo had offered to marry her and, if she accepted, that would go part-way towards completing the circle—but how could it be the same without love to bind them together?

'Peg? What's Dr da Cruz doing here?'

'He's cheering the Johnson girls up,' Peg said far too innocently as she glanced across the ward. 'With the two of them under the weather and their parents both working they need the extra attention.'

Maria could hardly argue with that but why was *Leo* the one doing the visiting? She'd been expecting to hear from him so that they could arrange to have their talk but for over a week there'd been no message and she'd begun to wonder if he *had* changed his mind after all.

Her pager bleeped as she was halfway across the ward and she had to leave the tall, dark-haired man sitting comfortably on the edge of one bed while he chatted easily to the two enthralled young girls.

It was her day on call again but at least this time the closest lift was working properly and it was easy enough to go backwards and forwards to the accident department without exhausting herself.

Luckily the awful lingering sickness seemed to have disappeared at last and, with it, the drained greyness of her face. At last she was able to look in the bathroom mirror and see that she was beginning to look more like her old self—just before she finally lost her figure.

The only trouble was that while she was steadily regaining all the weight she had lost the progress of her pregnancy meant that she was also feeling more and more exhausted by the end of each day, especially the days when she was on call and hardly had two minutes to sit still.

That afternoon it was especially frustrating, with Leo always just too far away for her to talk to him before she had to dash off somewhere else.

It wasn't until she was called back downstairs three times in succession without even reaching the ward in between that she began to admit to herself that Leo had been right.

'I can't go on like this,' she muttered breathlessly, her white coat flapping as she trod swiftly along the corridor towards the paediatric ward. Her stomach was complaining loudly that she hadn't fed it for far too long and she was beginning to feel distinctly light-headed.

'Here.' Peg held out a cup of tea and a slice of freshly buttered toast as she slipped back into the ward. It was almost as though she had known that Maria was on her way. 'Sit down and get that inside you before you end up on the floor again. At least, this time, the poor man wouldn't have so far to come. . .'

She stopped speaking but it was too late.

'It was you, wasn't it!' Maria pounced, speaking round a delicious mouthful before swallowing hurriedly. '*You* told him.'

'Well, *someone* had to.' Her chin came up defensively. 'He said you were heading for a disaster and he was right.'

'But. . .I thought you were my friend, Peg,' Maria said, her voice a mixture of puzzlement and hurt. 'Why did you have to tell him I'd collapsed?'

'*Because* I'm your friend,' she replied staunchly. 'You give so much to everyone else and never expect anything in return. When he asked me if I'd be willing to keep an eye on you I was only too glad that someone else cared about you too.'

Maria felt the swift sting of tears gathering and blinked hard to control them as she managed a watery smile. 'Ah, Peg, my friend. What would I do without you to. . .?'

She never finished the sentence as her pager cut in yet again with its shrill summons.

'*Enough*!' The deep voice startled her as it growled fiercely in her ear, two hands settling firmly on her shoulders to stop her getting up. 'You can just sit still and finish your tea while I take this call for you.' He straightened up and, out of the corner of her eye, Maria saw him take in Peg's bemused expression. 'Well. . .' he smiled roguishly in her direction '. . .I can't have my wife collapsing through overwork, can I?'

CHAPTER SIX

'WIFE?' Peg squeaked as soon as he left the room, her eyes growing enormous. 'And you thought *I'd* been keeping secrets!'

After its initial startled leap into her throat Maria's heart sank into her aching feet. She only had to look at her friend's expression to know that she wasn't going to be allowed to escape until Peg had heard everything.

The only trouble was that there was nothing to tell and she had a strong suspicion that Leo's parting comment had been a deliberate manoeuvre designed to force her hand.

'Come on, Maria,' Peg coaxed excitedly, 'tell me what's been going on. When did the two of you get married? Why didn't any of us know before now—or am I the last to know?'

The fleeting look of hurt in her friend's eyes made Maria want to curse out loud at autocratic Dr Leo da Cruz. How was she supposed to answer her? If she told Peg the truth it would make Leo look a fool for claiming that they were married but if she supported Leo's claim it could destroy her friend's trust in her.

'Sister Mulholland?' The tentative voice was accompanied by a knock on the partly opened door and Maria breathed a silent sigh of relief at her temporary reprieve when Jeremy Tolliver's mother answered the invitation to come in.

'Hello, Mrs Tolliver,' Maria greeted her with a

heartfelt smile. 'I'll just get out of your way.'

'I'm sorry to interrupt, Doctor.' The poor woman became flustered when she recognised the white coat. 'I can wait outside if you're busy talking to Sister.'

'No need.' Maria was on her feet. 'Sister Mulholland has just saved my life with a cup of tea and some toast so I've got no excuse not to get back to work now.'

As she left the room she looked back just long enough to wave silently to a frustrated Peg and mouth the word 'Later'.

Hidden in the depths of the pocket of her white coat she crossed her fingers in the hope that before she saw Peg again she'd have a chance to grab Leo by the throat and find out what game he was playing.

'Laura's been telling me about her leg-lengthener,' Leo told Maria as she joined him in the ward at the end of her shift, her coat and bag clutched in the crook of one arm.

He was smiling at the shy youngster and, as Maria watched, the pale blue eyes begin to sparkle with new light.

'Dr da Cruz said he hasn't seen one working before so I had to tell him how it works.'

'And did he understand?' Maria prompted, feeling guilty as she determinedly ignored the surreptitious beckoning signals she could see Peg making from the door of her office.

'He wanted to know why I only needed to have one leg done. He asked if I was going to live on the side of a hill so I needed one leg longer than the other.' She giggled as her cheeks became coloured a pretty pink.

'And then I thought it was because she wanted to

walk round in circles,' Leo added and Katy Johnson joined in her sister's laughter.

'I told him that I had my leg broken when I was pushed over by a bully just after I started at school,' Laura continued when she'd regained her breath. 'And when it was in plaster the other leg started growing so the broken one got left behind and it couldn't catch up.'

'And, then,' Katy joined in, determined not to be left out of the telling, 'they put her to sleep and one of the doctors broke her leg again.'

'Ah, but he put pins either side of the break to join it to the fixators, didn't he?' Maria smiled at the younger girl's gruesome delight in telling her part of the tale.

'And now we have to turn the screws one millimetre each day to stretch my bones where they're mending.' Laura pulled a face. 'It makes my leg ache like tooth-ache, especially after the physiotherapist makes me do my exercises to stretch my muscles.'

'I don't have to do fizzy-ferapy,' her little sister gloated with a grin.

'You will,' Laura warned. 'Won't she, Doctor? Otherwise her leg won't get strong again.'

'Then *Katy* might be the one walking round in circles,' Leo pointed out. 'Or she might have to move to a house on the side of a hill. . .'

There was the familiar sound of the ward doors open-ing and they all turned in time to watch Mr and Mrs Johnson hurry through.

'Mummy. Daddy,' the two girls chorused through their renewed laughter and Maria watched the worried expressions on their parents' faces disappear in an instant.

'Hello girls. Katy. Laura. You're looking happier this evening. . .'

Leo and Maria had moved aside so that the little family could share hugs and kisses and, with the briefest of farewells, Leo made their excuses and grabbed Maria by the elbow.

'Quick,' he muttered out of the corner of his mouth, 'before Peg sees you're free,' and they scooted out of the ward door like a pair of truants.

'Hey, slow down.' Maria panted to a halt when they turned the corner by the lifts.

'I'm sorry.' Leo was immediately penitent, apologising under his breath as they joined the small knot of people so that his voice wouldn't carry. 'I'd forgotten about the baby.'

'It's got nothing to do with the baby.' Maria whispered the words fiercely as the doors slid shut, thankfully enclosing the two of them in a private box for the few seconds it would take to reach the ground floor. 'My legs aren't as long as yours. And, anyway,' she added, 'it was your fault we're running away from Peg in the first place. What on earth possessed you to say such a thing?'

'You mean about getting married?' He raised one dark eyebrow imperiously.

'You implied that I was already your *wife*,' Maria reminded him breathlessly as he hurried her out of the lift and across the reception area. 'How could you say something like that when we haven't even had time to talk about it, let alone make a decision?'

'Well, it was only a little premature. You *will* be my wife as soon as we can arrange it.' The words were reaching her over his shoulder as they made their way towards his car, his tone as decisive as ever until he abruptly turned to face her in the middle of the consultants' car park and took her hands in his, capturing her with his shadowy silver gaze. 'Won't you, Maria?'

It was the first time that Maria had seen him show a sign of uncertainty and suddenly she realised that the revelation of this facet of his character had just sealed her fate.

Just those few words spoken in that hesitant husky voice had made her realise that she was falling in love with him—this outwardly contained, self-confident man whose intimidating manner hid a battered heart of gold which only his patients were allowed to know.

'Yes,' she whispered, knowing that there was no longer anything to think about. She wanted to be with this man who was the father of her unborn child for however long she could. 'Yes.' Her voice was stronger now that the decision had been made. 'I'll marry you, Leo.'

All the way home the cacophony in her head grew louder as doubt piled on doubt.

She'd just agreed to marry Leo but what did she know about him? Only the barest minimum, apart from his excellent professional reputation added to what she'd seen of him with her own eyes in his time at St Augustine's.

By the time he drew up outside her flat in Alma Road she was shaking, convinced that she must have lost her mind. Just because she had realised that she was falling in love with him was no reason to suppose that he had changed *his* mind about anything.

A sudden black thought struck her and she tensed in horror, feeling the blood drain from her face just as he opened her door and offered her a helping hand.

'Maria? What's the matter?' He crouched down beside the open door so that he could see her more clearly, his hand automatically reaching for her wrist and checking her pulse. 'It's racing. . . Are you feeling ill?'

She shook her head dumbly, unable to voice the awful thoughts which filled her head.

'Can you move?' He released her seat belt, his arm almost enclosing her in an embrace as he reached across her for the catch. 'We'd better get you inside.'

Maria felt like an old lady as he supported her all the way into her sitting-room. She was furious to find that she couldn't even control her fingers well enough to unfasten the buttons on her coat and had to stand like a helpless child while he took it off for her.

The whole time one strong arm was wrapped around her shoulders until she was safely seated in her favourite chair.

'You need a cup of tea,' he decided and whisked her coat away to hang it up before she heard him moving about in her kitchen.

While she listened to him setting cups out on the tray she concentrated on breathing deeply and slowly, pleased to feel her pulse rate grow steadier and the tremor in her hands calm down until it was barely noticeable——until Leo came back into the room.

'Here.' He moved a small table beside her chair and carefully placed her cup within easy reach. 'I suppose recent events finally caught up with you,' he said with an understanding air.

If only that was true, Maria thought as she flicked a nervous glance towards him. What would he say if he knew the real reason I've got a fit of the shakes? She reached out for the cup, carefully cradling it between her palms as she absorbed the warmth and gratefully accepting the brief respite before she had to voice her fears.

'When would be the best time to organise this wedding?' His deep voice broke into her muddled musings. 'Have you got a couple of days off in the near future or will we just have to take our chances on getting away together later on?'

Maria found herself silently shaking her head, unable to think about dates and time away when her head was still too full of panic.

'I don't. . .I can't. . . Oh, Leo, I don't think we're doing the right thing. . .' She looked up at him fearfully, expecting an explosion but he began laughing softly.

'I think you've got a bad case of cold feet.' He smiled easily, his voice calm and unworried. 'I promise it will all be all right. We've got so much in common that. . .'

'How do you know?' the words burst out of her. 'You don't know anything about me. Not really. So, how can you possibly know that everything will be all right?'

'But, Maria. . .' She ignored his attempted interruption and forged on.

'It was only a few weeks ago that you were determined to go to court to force me into having tests done on the baby to try to make me have an abortion.' She could hear the shrill tone to her voice but she was no longer in control, the words spilling over like water out of a breached dam.

'*Now* you're saying that we're going to be successful at playing happy families just because we work in the same field of medicine and have so much in common. It's such a radical about-face that it makes me wonder if you've got an ulterior motive behind all your tender attention.'

She ended the accusation with a glare and saw the invisible shutters come down to hide his startled expression. For just a fleeting second she thought that she'd seen hurt in his eyes but it was the brief blaze of anger which had lingered longest before he ruthlessly controlled it.

'And what motive might that be?' he said quietly, the air in the room seeming to grow chilly around her.

'Well, how should I know?' she blustered, already regretting her outburst. 'First you say you don't want to get married, then you do; then you say you don't want the baby and the next moment you're going to take care of it—or are you. . .?' She left the final words hanging in the air.

'And what, exactly, do you mean by that?' he said very precisely, his eyes spearing her like twin lasers as he sat as immobile as a bronze statue.

'Perhaps it was just a coincidence that soon after I threaten to deny that you're the baby's father you suddenly came up with the idea of marriage. You can hardly deny that if we were married it would give you far greater legal power over what happens to the baby.'

'So,' he acknowledged coldly, his face drawn into a scornful mask, 'you think I suggested that we get married so that I would have a better chance of forcing you into having the baby tested?'

'It's perfectly logical,' Maria said defensively, quivering in the face of his obvious fury.

'I suppose it is—apart from one fundamental fact.'

There was a sting in his voice like the lash of a whip as he spoke. 'Even if I *did* want to force you into having the baby tested as soon as we were married there would be no point because it would now be illegal to perform an abortion.'

Maria felt sick.

She had completely forgotten that time had been marching on at an alarming rate while she'd waited for Leo to contact her—all she had been worried about was *why* he hadn't spoken to her. It hadn't occurred to her to remember that she had now entered the third trimester of her pregnancy.

If only she'd taken a moment to think things through before she'd spoken. . .but she'd been too panic-stricken at the sudden realisation that she'd become so emotionally vulnerable; too afraid that she was racing blindly into a relationship too fast to see the pitfalls.

'I'm sorry,' she whispered. 'Oh, Leo, I. . .'

'At least we won't be going into this arrangement with our eyes shut,' he said crisply as he stood up and fished in his pockets for his car keys. 'Although I must admit I hadn't realised you thought me quite so devious.'

'No,' she cried, suddenly scared. He was so angry— angry enough to walk out of her life? 'Leo, please let me. . .'

'Don't worry about it, Maria,' he interrupted as he tossed the small bunch of keys up in the air and caught them again with a vicious swipe of his hand. 'As you said, we don't know a great deal about each other but at least we'll have had the opportunity to remedy that by the time the baby arrives—that's if you still want to go ahead?'

Maria gazed numbly at his composed face but there was no expression there to give her a clue as to his own feelings.

All she knew was that he was more important to her than any other man in her life and she had hurt him deeply with her suggestion that he would have married her just to have the power to decide the baby's fate.

'Yes,' she whispered, her eyes falling to her entwined fingers lying so still and silent in her lap, hoping to hide the gathering moisture behind her thick dark lashes. 'I still want to go ahead.'

'Good,' he said briskly, as though this was some mundane business discussion drawing to a close. 'If you let me know when you're next due for some time off I'll make the arrangements. Any preference as to where it takes place?'

For just a second she had a mental vision of the wedding she had once dreamt of, the way most young girls do—of walking up the aisle in a white dress to join the man she loved. . .

'Well. . .' She paused. Old dreams died hard. 'Would you have any objection. . .? No.' She shook her head dismissively.

'What?' he demanded.

'It doesn't matter—I'd forgotten for a moment that you'd been married before.'

'What difference does that make? Ah—' he suddenly realised the significance '—you wanted a church blessing?'

'It doesn't matter. The registry office will probably be able to fit it in more easily.' She hid her disappointment behind logic.

He was silent for a moment, the power of his gaze

reaching her right across the room, before he gave a little nod as if he'd come to a decision.

'Right, then. As soon as you let me have a list of suggested dates I'll get back to you and let you know which one.'

He left her sitting in her chair feeling as if she'd been run over by a juggernaut, her brain so scrambled that she couldn't think straight.

'Where are we going?' Maria fished inside her cuff for her handkerchief and wiped her hands. She didn't dare touch the skirt of the outfit Leo had insisted on buying for her or the beautiful ivory-coloured fabric might spoil. 'Isn't the registry office back the other way?'

'Don't worry about it,' Leo said calmly, capturing one clammy hand between the warm strength of his and pressing it reassuringly. 'I'm sure the cabbie knows where he's taking us.'

'But what if we're late? Would the registrar wait for us?' There were a million butterflies in her stomach and the baby must be reacting to her tension because she was certain that she was going to have bruised ribs from the frantic activity going on inside her.

'Maria.' He hooked one lean finger under her chin and tilted her face up so that she was looking straight into his silvery grey gaze. 'There isn't going to be a problem so relax.'

'I'm sorry, Leo. It's just. . .I'm still not sure we're doing the right thing. . .'

'Shh. . .'

He touched her lips with the tip of one finger and she went silent, savouring the gentle contact.

'You look beautiful and everything will go

smoothly,' he repeated as the car slowed down.

She missed the warmth of his finger when he took his hand away and turned hurriedly to hide the wash of heat in her cheeks, gazing blankly out at the building they were drawing up outside.

'Leo? What are we doing here? What's happening?' She stared out of the window in bewilderment then looked back at him. 'We've stopped outside a church. *My* church. . .'

'This was what you really wanted. . .wasn't it?' His dark brows were drawn together as an uncertain expression filled his eyes.

'Oh, Leo, yes.' A fragile smile trembled on her lips as she suddenly realised what he had done. She had no idea how he'd managed to arrange it, especially in such a short time, but her heart filled with pleasure that he'd even thought of trying. 'Oh, yes. This is what I wanted.'

'Well, then. What are we waiting for?' He reached forward and flung the car door open then turned back to help her to the path. 'We've got an important appointment in there so let's get moving!'

Suddenly her heart felt as light as a helium-filled balloon and, tucking her hand in the crook of his arm, she walked beside him into the little church.

It wasn't until hours later that her head stopped spinning long enough to sort out all the impressions that had bombarded her as they'd walked together into a church full of guests.

Peg had been waiting for them just inside the door with a spray of freesias and fern and Leo's friend, Andreas, had arrived from Italy in time to stand up as his best man. She didn't have time to look at the rest of the guests in the few seconds it took to reach the altar steps, their faces just a blur as she walked the short distance at Leo's side.

And then they didn't matter. As far as Maria was concerned, she and Leo could have been the only two in the church as she concentrated on the heart-stirring promises they were making to each other.

In the brief pause after Leo was told that he could kiss his new bride she wondered mistily if fate would be kind enough to make him fall in love with her, too, but then his hands were on her shoulders as he turned her to face him.

'Hello, Dr da Cruz,' he whispered intimately, his grey eyes very serious as his glance roved over her face.

'Hello, Dr da Cruz,' she returned as a smile blossomed under the touch of his eyes. She was certain that her feelings must be as obvious as words on the open pages of a book but then he was concentrating on her mouth.

Although it had been months ago that she'd experienced them, she remembered all too clearly what his kisses were like and her lips tingled in anticipation so that the tip of her tongue flicked out to moisten them.

'Maria,' he murmured with a tiny groan as he touched his lips to hers and her heart leapt at the contained passion in his voice.

His arms slid round her shoulders and pulled her into the sheltering curve of his body. As her softness yielded to the hard-muscled power of his lean frame the gentle swell of her belly pressed against him just as the baby gave an enormous kick.

Leo tensed as if he'd been stung, his eyes suddenly dark with comprehension as they gazed down into hers.

Under the cover of her edge-to-edge jacket he slid

one hand over her and was immediately rewarded with
another violent contortion of the little person contained inside.

'And hello to you, too, baby da Cruz,' he whispered
and Maria's heart sank when she saw the solemn
expression on his face.

How could she have allowed herself to forget the
reason why this marriage was taking place?

As Leo released her and stepped back the organist
began the first few bars of Maria's favourite hymn but
all the excitement and anticipation had gone, even when
he took her hand and led her through to the sacristy to
sign the register with Peg and Andreas as witnesses.

At a small hotel nearby Leo stood with his arm around
her shoulders as they greeted their guests but this time
she knew better than to allow herself to think foolish
thoughts about love and for ever. This time she knew
that the gesture was just for the benefit of their guests.

When she'd seen them in the church it had looked
as if there were dozens of them, especially as Maria
had expected to find just their two witnesses waiting
at the local registry office.

She had already counted twenty people when Leo's
arm tightened reflexively around her and she glanced
towards the latecomers just entering the room.

'Theo. Sophia,' he said coldly to the elegant couple
who stood in front of them, every inch of his bearing
telling Maria that he didn't want them here.

She shifted briefly in his hold and he seemed to
remember that she was beside him, his fingers stroking
her shoulder almost in apology as he lessened the
pressure of his arm.

'Maria. May I introduce my brother Theo and his wife Sophia?'

Maria had known from his startling good looks that Theo must be some relative of Leo's but, although he might be aesthetically more handsome than his brother, he didn't have the indefinable aura of power that made Leo stand out in a crowd.

Sophia, too, was beautiful, uncannily like a *haute couture* picture, everything about her so perfect that when she turned towards Leo Maria almost expected her to be a cardboard cut-out just millimetres thick.

'Leo, darling,' she greeted him in a saccharine voice, her smile never reaching her coldly calculating eyes. 'When Andreas told us you were getting married we just had to be here to wish you well.'

There was nothing overt in anything that the three of them had said or done but there was a terrible tension between them, the atmosphere so electric that Maria quite expected to see sparks fly.

'Thank you,' she murmured politely, taking the initiative when she realised that Leo wasn't going to reply. 'I'm glad you could be with us today. If you'd like to go over to the other side of the room there's a drink waiting for you.'

She watched a strange expression cross Sophia's face when Leo calmly allowed his new wife to dismiss the two of them but, although her perfectly painted mouth tightened into a hard straight line, with a room full of other guests waiting to speak to Leo and Maria there was nothing she could do but take her leave of them.

'Leo?' Maria had waited until they were finally alone for a minute before she spoke in an undertone, keeping a smile on her face for the benefit of their guests. 'What's the matter? Didn't they let you know they were coming?'

'I deliberately didn't invite them,' he said through gritted teeth, his eyes as cold and hard as granite.

'But. . .? He's your brother. . .' Maria was puzzled. There had obviously been more than a passing argument between them—something far more serious. But what. . .?

'And she's my ex-wife,' he said in arctic tones.

Now Maria understood the tension between the three of them. This was the woman who'd borne Leo a son and then, even though her medical knowledge had told her that he needed special care, had knowingly neglected him until he was so weakened by the disease he'd inherited that he'd died on his birthday in his father's arms.

'Well.' She threaded her fingers through his and gripped his hand tightly as she spoke, her voice calm and quiet enough just to reach his ears. 'It would give their presence today far more importance than it warrants if we bothered to throw them out.' She tilted her chin to meet the chilly grey of his eyes with the warmth of her own, a fugitive smile lifting the corners of her mouth.

'After all your hard work I'm not going to let anything spoil today so let's just make our way around the room talking to the people you *did* invite.'

He gazed silently into her eyes for long seconds before a smile creased the tiny lines at the corner of his eyes.

'That sounds like an excellent idea.' He leaned forward to deposit a brief kiss on the end of her nose.

'Let's start off as we mean to go on, concentrating on the important things in life—like champagne. . .'

He reached out towards the tray carried by a passing waiter and relieved him of two glasses.

'Leo. . .?' she began doubtfully but he shook his head.

'One glass, sipped slowly, won't do the baby any harm. It might even send the little blighter to sleep so you can enjoy some food without indigestion.'

He chimed their glasses and they drank together, their eyes focused intently on each other almost as though they were making a pact with each other in spite of the circumstances of their marriage.

'Hey, you two,' Peg's voice broke teasingly into the silent communion. 'You ought to be circulating so we all get a chance to speak to you. There'll be plenty of time for gazing soulfully at each other when we're gone.'

'Peg!' Maria muttered, mortified that several of the other guests had overheard and were chuckling at her humourously outspoken comments.

'Sister Mulholland.' Leo bowed gravely in her direction. 'We stand corrected.' He looked across the room and beckoned to his friend. 'I must introduce you to Andreas.'

'Oh, there's no need. . .' Peg began and Maria had to hide a smile when she saw the heightened colour in her friend's cheeks as Leo made the introductions.

His best man was about the same age as Peg and looked devastating in his dark suit and white shirt but the thing which caught Maria's eye was the intensity with which he listened to Peg when she spoke and the unmistakable interest in his eyes as he surreptitiously took in how well she looked in her elegant new outfit.

Later she would have to ask Leo if there was any chance of matchmaking. Whether he thought that *his* friend might be a suitable match for *her* friend.

They continued around the room, spending time with each of their guests, the new ease between herself and Leo allowing her to smile openly.

Unfortunately Maria was also uncomfortably aware that, although they seemed to be taking care not to allow their paths to cross, Theo and Sophia were following them the whole time with their eyes.

Finally Maria couldn't put off a visit to the bathroom any longer.

'I think it must have been the champagne,' she murmured to Leo. 'It's gone straight through me.'

'Not very comfortable in view of the activity of a certain little lodger.' He smiled wryly.

The facilities were quite sumptuous and Maria paused a moment before she rejoined Leo and their guests to take advantage of the well-lit mirror over the basin to tidy her hair and renew her lipstick.

One disadvantage of the fact that she hadn't had a hand in the planning of the event meant that she had no idea how much longer it would be before their guests started to leave.

Leo hadn't said whether they were going to be transferring their belongings straight away or leaving the job until the morning. Now that she came to think of it they hadn't even decided whose home they were going to be living in. All he had told her was that she wasn't on duty this evening.

She took a half-step back from the mirror to take a look at the overall picture she made, pleased to see how much better she was looking these days. Her dark hair was gleaming with good health and her eyes were bright with happiness now that some of her uncertainty had been relieved.

She was just straightening the front edges of her jacket, enjoying the sumptuous feel of the supple ivory silk between her fingers, when the door opened behind her and she glanced up at the reflection.

Her heart began to thump uncomfortably as she saw Sophia walk in, dark eyes settling on Maria as though she'd expected to find her there, her whole bearing full of the tension she was trying to hide.

'So,' she drawled as she leant back against the door. Her pose was apparently nonchalant but Maria recognised that she had positioned herself deliberately, preventing anyone else from joining them. 'Leo finally managed to get someone else to marry him. Oh—' she covered her brightly painted mouth with matching talons in feigned remorse '—I suppose he *has* told you that I was your predecessor.'

'Of course,' Maria said as calmly as though the whole topic was boring. 'He's told me everything.' Without turning, she had managed to fix Sophia's gaze in the mirror and she saw her grow pale.

'Well,' her tone grew venomous, 'with a name like yours and your colouring it's odds-on your family's from the Mediterranean region so I hope you've had all your blood tests done.'

'Of course.' Maria had a feeling that she knew what was coming next and busied herself putting away her lipstick and closing her bag before she turned to face her. 'Didn't you know that Leo and I met as a result of our work with children who have the inherited anaemias?'

'What about you?' Sophia probed, her eyes narrowed into glittering slits. 'Do you carry any of the traits?'

'Beta thalassaemia,' she confirmed quietly. 'I had a brother who died of beta thalassaemia major.'

'Well, you'd better make sure you don't get pregnant or you'll be risking losing a child of your own as well— Leo *has* told you that he's a carrier, hasn't he?'

'Of course,' Maria repeated. 'He told me about his son, too.' She caught hold of the edge of her loose jacket and pulled it aside, curving her hand deliberately over the cleverly concealing folds of her outfit to reveal the growing evidence of the child inside her. 'But obviously some things are worth taking a chance over. . .'

She'd thrown the words at Sophia like a challenge, secure in the knowledge that her new sister-in-law would never hear the true story behind her pregnancy. To her surprise she watched the perfectly made-up face drain of colour, the artful shading over her cheek-bones standing out grotesquely as her dark gaze stared with glassy-eyed horror.

'Oh, God,' she whispered, her eyes like ugly bruises in her white face. 'Oh, my God.' She scrabbled for the handle behind her, apparently unable to drag her eyes away until the last moment as she stumbled her way out of the room, the door sighing softly shut behind her.

CHAPTER SEVEN

'WHAT happened in there?' Leo muttered when she finally rejoined him.

'In where?' Maria stalled for time, still unable to understand why Sophia had reacted the way she had to the revelation that she and Leo were expecting a baby. Although she would have preferred to have been married before she started a family, Maria was well aware that her situation was hardly the sort of occurrence to cause so much shock.

'Maria.' There was a warning in his tone. 'Peg tried to go after Sophia when she followed you but the door was blocked. Then, a couple of minutes later, Sophia came out of there as if she had a devil on her tail. She grabbed Theo and dragged him out of the hotel without so much as waving goodbye.'

'Well, it certainly hasn't been a boring afternoon,' she began brightly, only to subside when Leo glowered at her. 'All right. If you must know, she introduced herself as your ex-wife—just in case you hadn't told me—and warned me not to get pregnant.'

'And?' he prompted, obviously knowing that there was more.

'I showed her my bump and I thought she was going to pass out but before I could say anything she was gone.' A sudden thought struck her. 'Do you think it brought it all back to her? Losing her own child? Was she worried for us?'

'Unlikely,' Leo snorted. 'The only person who matters to Sophia is Sophia.'

'So, we won't be seeing much of them?' In spite of the discomfort of the situation she couldn't help a trace of wistfulness creeping into her voice. Ever since Marco had died she'd had an unsatisfied longing to belong to a family. . .

'They don't spend much time in England. Theo's the chief executive officer of the family holdings in Italy and Greece and the lifestyle over there suits Sophia better.'

Having seen the way the woman dressed, Maria could well believe that her social life was normally somewhat different to this intimate wedding reception.

'In that case I don't understand.' She shook her head. 'I can't see why the two of them even bothered to come, especially as they weren't invited. Then, when she deliberately followed me to speak to me, I thought she was genuinely worried that I might not know that you were carrying beta thalassaemia trait but her reaction to the baby was. . .well, it was weird.' She pulled a face and laughed when he tapped his finger on the end of her screwed-up nose.

'That's not important now.' He smiled down into her dark honey eyes. How could she ever have thought his silvery grey eyes cold? They carried all the heat of molten metal. . .

He flicked a glance at the slim watch circling his wrist.

'It's time to go, Dr da Cruz,' he announced, raising one hand to attract Peg's attention.

'Do we have to go so soon?' She was conscious of a feeling of disappointment. Until that strange episode with Sophia she'd been thoroughly enjoying the unexpected party—the whole unexpectedly magical day.

'If we're going to get to the hotel in time for a meal this evening, we do.'

'Hotel?' The leap of pleasure at the thought that there were still some surprises in store for the day brought the smile back to her face. 'You let me think we were going to be doing removals this evening!'

'Hey!' Peg arrived, closely followed by Andreas, just as Maria thumped Leo's arm in retribution.

'I don't think you're supposed to start beating him before you leave the wedding reception,' the best man's attractively accented voice was accompanied by a wide grin. 'It won't do his macho reputation any good.'

'You Latin men!' Peg exclaimed hotly. 'Surely it's more important to have a good reputation with those who know you than to preserve appearances with people who don't matter!'

'Ah, but who's to know which chance acquaintance would have turned out to be someone important in your life if only you hadn't blotted your copybook with them on first meeting?' Andreas picked up Peg's hand and ostentatiously kissed the back of her fingers. 'It could be those first impressions which make all the difference, couldn't it?'

Maria knew that Leo's friend was only bantering with Peg, the way a man does when he meets a woman who sparks his interest, but she felt her cheeks grow warm as his words struck a personal chord.

Who could tell how the relationship between Leo and herself might have developed if they had been introduced to each other as colleagues on the first day of the conference?

As it was she was afraid that whenever he looked at her he would always remember that when he'd first seen her he had thought she was a prostitute; had believed that she was willing to sleep with him because Andreas had paid for her time. . .

'Maria?' Leo's deep voice broke into her unhappy thoughts. 'Are you feeling all right?'

They had decided not to tell any of her colleagues about her pregnancy until after the wedding so she was grateful for his careful choice of words.

He wrapped one strong arm around her shoulders and she allowed herself to lean against him, drawing comfort from the contact even though she knew it was all for show.

'I'm fine.' She smiled up at him, her eyes travelling over his handsome face in open enjoyment, secure in the knowledge that the guests would see what they expected to see—a new wife in love with her husband.

It was ironic that the only one who wouldn't believe it was Leo. He would be convinced that she was merely playing a part for their audience.

'Andreas?' Leo's call drew his friend's liquid gaze reluctantly from Peg's flustered face. 'Have you ordered the car?'

'It should be waiting on the forecourt already,' he confirmed. 'All you've got to do is make your farewells and you're on your way.'

'Well, then.' Leo put a guiding hand to the small of Maria's back to usher her towards the door.

They passed the scant remains of the sumptuous buffet and Leo reached out for the small package the hotel caterers had left in readiness for him beside the elegant stand which had held their beautiful cake.

'Peg's suggestion,' Leo said as he held it up. 'She said that the bride and groom never have the chance to enjoy the food at their reception so the caterer saved some cake for us.'

'I suppose those are the emergency rations in case we don't reach the hotel in time for a meal tonight!' Maria teased under the cover of the calls of good wishes which surrounded them as they reached the door.

'Oh!' She stopped suddenly and turned to face the happy throng. 'I nearly forgot. . .' She drew back her arm and flung her bouquet over the heads of the assembled group.

One long, dark-suited arm rose out of the reaching forest to pluck it in mid-flight and Maria saw Andreas smile wickedly as he presented his trophy to a furiously blushing Peg before Leo finally managed to escort her out to the waiting car.

'Are we going back to my flat to pick up some things first or will we do that after we've been to the hospital?' Maria had sunk blissfully into the soft upholstery, grateful that at last she could take her weight off her feet. She'd hardly regained her pre-pregnancy weight but her feet were complaining as though she was carrying an elephant around.

'Neither,' Leo murmured as he angled himself towards her, his long legs taking full advantage of the space in the back of the taxi as he leant back into the corner. 'Peg took care of your packing.'

'But. . .'

'Her original idea was to pick up a new toothbrush for each of us from the shop in the hospital foyer,' he continued with a twinkle in his eyes, 'but I pointed out that it was always a good idea to take some sort of robe as well—in case of emergencies.'

For several seconds Maria was speechless, her eyes fixed hungrily on his lean body as her mind was flooded with images of spending the night with him in a hotel bedroom with no more luggage than a new toothbrush. She suddenly realised that he was watching her expression and her cheeks instantly grew warm.

'But we *are* going to go to the hospital before we go on to the hotel, aren't we?' she said confidently, desperate to distract him from his present train of thought. 'I need to check up on one of my special children and the little boy who came in last night with. . .'

'It's all taken care of, Maria,' he broke in, then reached out to capture her hand while she spluttered indignantly, lacing his fingers comfortingly between hers. 'It won't be a problem. Ian was only too happy to oblige and Ross agreed that you needed a couple of days. . .'

'A couple. . .? You spoke to Ross MacFadden without telling me?' She drew in a horrified breath as she visualised the consultant's reaction. She knew only too well that he wasn't noted for his respect and consideration towards the female members of his staff. 'Now there's no way he'll ever write me a decent reference when I want to go for a consultancy.'

'On the contrary,' Leo soothed, gripping her hand tighter when she would have snatched it out of his grasp, 'he had some very complimentary things to say about your dedication to the job.'

'He. . .did?' She subsided incredulously, all the

wind taken out of her sails. 'I've never heard him say anything nice about anyone.'

Leo leant towards her as though he was going to tell her a secret. 'It might have had something to do with my volunteering my services for a presentation at the series of lectures he's giving,' he murmured with a chuckle.

'That's bribery,' Maria objected in mock outrage.

'Who cares if it got us what we wanted?' He brought her hand up to press a kiss on her knuckles and she felt the warmth go right through her.

'Did we?' she whispered, her eyes growing wider as they were caught in the clear silver of his gaze, her brain becoming impossibly scrambled by his nearness.

'Of course we did,' he confirmed as he repeated the kiss on each of her slender knuckles. 'We couldn't invite all those people to our wedding without going on a honeymoon, could we?'

Maria shivered as his meaning dawned on her and leant back into her corner of the seat so that she broke the contact between them.

She had so nearly been tempted into believing that he had arranged for the two of them to have a weekend together because he *wanted* to go away with her. Thank heavens he had reminded her in time that the whole event was just a charade being played out for their friends and colleagues before she had a chance to say something to embarrass both of them.

As the taxi drew up outside the front door of the hotel a little while later Maria thought that she couldn't have imagined a hotel more different from the one in Italy where she and Leo had first encountered each other.

Where the other one had been quite grand and the rooms they'd occupied sumptuous, this one was cosy, with low beamed ceilings and uneven floors covered by antique carpets.

'It's like something out of a story-book,' she exclaimed in a nervous voice once they'd been shown to their room, her gaze fixed firmly out of the window. 'It looks as if it's old enough to be Jacobean at least.'

'Well, I hope the mattress is a little newer than that!' Leo teased, finally drawing her eyes back to the four-poster bed which dominated the room.

She'd been transfixed by her first sight of it, blocking the doorway as her feet refused to take her any further into the room until Leo's presence behind her had forced her to enter.

In a panic she'd made an unnecessarily thorough inspection of the rest of the room and its tiny adjoining bathroom, finally resorting to looking out into the dusk at the nearly invisible view to avoid looking at the bed again.

'Maria. . .'

'Is it getting very late? Surely it's time we went down for our meal?' She found herself gabbling in her nervousness, edging her way around the room to make her escape when Leo started walking towards her.

'Maria.' One lean hand appeared in front of her face, holding the solid wood door closed when she would have pulled it open.

She froze, hardly daring to breathe as she felt the warmth of his body so close behind her.

'Please, Maria, turn around.'

The soft words persuaded her to turn towards him even though she wasn't sure what he wanted.

'What are you afraid of? That the sight of a bed will make me leap on you?' One dark eyebrow was raised quizzically.

'I'm not exactly. . .afraid,' she murmured evasively. She was too nervous to hold his gaze in case her true feelings were as obvious as she feared. Unfortunately when she looked away her eyes encountered the rich splendour of the tapestry curtains draping the bed behind him and she didn't know where to direct her eyes.

'Well, if you aren't afraid what *is* the matter?' His fingers cupped her chin and turned her back to face the quicksilver intensity of his eyes.

'I suppose I'm embarrassed,' she burst out suddenly, knowing that she had to give him an answer even if it wasn't the *whole* answer.

'Embarrassed?' he repeated. 'About what?'

'About the situation. . .you and me. . .everything!'

'Well, that's pretty comprehensive. Could you try to be a little more specific?'

'No. . . Yes. . . Well, *look* at me!' she wailed and pulled a face as she gestured down at herself.

'I've been looking at you ever since I picked you up to take you to the church,' he murmured. His expression softened as his eyes travelled over her from the dark curls framing her delicate face, skimming over the creamy fabric of her outfit and down to the elegant matching shoes on her slender feet. 'Beautiful,' he added in a husky voice.

'But I'm pregnant!' She gestured impatiently towards her elegantly camouflaged waist, all too conscious that the last couple of weeks had at last seen a marked increase in her waistline.

'Beautifully pregnant,' he began soothingly, taking her hand to lead her towards a softly upholstered chair. 'The last few weeks you've really begun to look so much better—much healthier. . .'

'Oh, Leo! You don't understand!' She batted his hand away angrily and stomped across the carpet before she turned back to face him from the safety of the other side of the room.

'I'm over seven months pregnant and I'm on my honeymoon with a man I've never seen.' She threw the words at him like an accusation, then found herself worrying her lower lip between her teeth as she waited for his reply.

'What do you mean?' His forehead was pleated into a frown. 'Is this an example of hormones scrambling your brain during pregnancy?'

'Don't be patronising,' she snapped, planting one fist on each hip belligerently. 'It's obvious what I mean—you just have to look at me.'

His frown grew deeper as he shook his head.

'Oh, for heaven's sake!' She threw her hands up in the air. 'We've made this baby but we've never even seen each other naked.'

The final word seemed to reverberate around the room for hours as she folded her arms defensively across her body.

'That's not quite true.'

His quiet words stopped her breath in her throat and the reminiscent smile which followed them nearly stopped her heart too.

'W-what do you. . .? When have you. . .?' The words wouldn't come.

'When I woke up that morning.' He answered the

question she couldn't frame. 'You were still fast asleep, your hair spread out across the pillow like strands of ebony silk. . .'

His voice had sunk to a husky murmur and she was mesmerised by the intensity of his gaze.

'The sun was slanting through a gap in the curtains and falling across your body, painting it with liquid gold. I'd never seen anything so beautiful before. . .'

'Oh, God.' Maria covered her face with her hands. 'That makes everything worse.'

'Because I saw you and you haven't seen me?' he questioned with a wry smile as he reached for his tie. 'If that's the problem it's easily remedied.'

'No!' She shook her head wildly. 'Because you saw me then when I was. . .was pretty and now I'm all. . . pregnant!' She whirled round and sped towards the seclusion of the compact bathroom but he moved faster, blocking her way effortlessly.

'Maria, Maria,' he crooned as he cupped her shoulders with his palms and massaged the tense muscles at the angle of her neck with sensitive fingertips. 'I know this is very awkward—for both of us. And I apologise for being so slow to understand your concerns.'

She drew in a deep breath and let it out in a heavy sigh as she leant tiredly back against the frame of the door. 'Where do we go from here, then?' she said uncertainly. 'It's still more than two months until the baby's born and we can hardly go round pretending it's not there. . .'

'But I *can* make sure I give you enough space to make you feel comfortable.'

'How?' Her eyes flew to the bed behind him. With only one bed in the room. . .

'Easily.' He smiled reassuringly. 'Until you feel more comfortable with the situation I just have to make sure that you have plenty of time to yourself first thing in the morning and last thing at night.'

'But. . . Wouldn't it be easier if you just asked if they've got another room for you or. . .or a room with twin beds?'

As she watched his smile faded and his eyes emptied of expression.

'I didn't realise you distrusted me so much,' he said coolly. His lips were tight with displeasure and Maria suddenly realised that she had hurt him deeply.

'If that's what you would prefer,' he continued, turning towards the door.

'No.' She grabbed his sleeve as he started to move away. 'I'm sorry. I'm being stupid. . . It must be those mood swings I was warned about. . .' she offered apologetically then stopped, her eyes fixed on his as she mentally crossed her fingers. 'The. . .the bed's plenty big enough for the two of us. It's. . .it's not as if either of us is any great size—yet!'

There was a long silence as his eyes probed hers and she tried to fill them with the apology he would never accept—the apology for hurting his male pride.

'Well,' he said finally, clearing his throat before he continued, 'if you'll give me a minute in the bathroom I'll get out of your way so that you can take your time.' He stepped past her and she noticed with a sinking heart that he made certain that he didn't touch her on his way. 'I can wait for you in the lounge until you're ready to come down for dinner,' he added in a toneless voice.

'Damn. Damn. Damn,' Maria muttered angrily as

soon as she heard the latch of the bathroom door click into place behind him. She had been concentrating so hard on her own embarrassment at the prospect of sharing the room with him that she hadn't realised how insulting the implication of her words would be.

The *last* thing she'd wanted to do was hurt him, especially now that she'd realised just how much she was coming to care for him.

She turned to the small weekend case which had been deposited on the gleaming wood of the linen chest at the foot of the bed and twisted the locks open.

The case was hers—she hadn't even realised it was missing; hadn't even thought to look for it when she didn't know that Leo was arranging for the two of them to go away together. But while she recognised the piece of luggage as the same one that had accompanied her on that fateful trip to Italy she didn't recognise the clothing lying inside it.

'What on earth. . .?' She gingerly lifted out a fragile drift of silky chiffon and it slithered like a midnight blue waterfall to hang in softly gleaming folds from the slender spaghetti straps in her hands. 'Where did *this* come from?'

She caught sight of a flash out of the corner of her eye as a silvery gift tag fluttered to the floor and she bent to retrieve it.

'Happy honeymoon. Enjoy!' she read, followed by Peg's familiar signature.

'Oh, Peg. You idiot.' The fond words were half laugh, half sob as she remembered that even her closest friend at St Augustine's didn't know the full story behind this apparently fairy-tale wedding.

In spite of her preoccupation she heard the sound of

water draining from the basin and she just had time to thrust the incriminating item under the nearest pillow as the bathroom door opened.

'See you later,' Leo confirmed as he made his way towards the door with hardly a glance in her direction. 'Take your time.'

'Take my time?' Maria muttered at the door when he closed it gently behind him, her stomach growling hungrily into the quiet of the room. 'Not likely! I'm starving!'

It was less than five minutes before she was following Leo down to the ground floor, her make-up hastily retouched and her hair released from bondage and given a thorough brushing to lie in a gleaming mantle over the ivory shoulders of her wedding outfit.

She paused as she entered the room, her eyes flicking around the cosy groups of armchairs and settees to find Leo. As her eyes fastened on him in a secluded corner she surprised a startled expression on his face as he watched her walk towards him. Maria felt an answering leap and her hopes rose again that everything would be all right.

'That was quick,' he commented blandly as he stood up and Maria had to stifle a groan of disappointment as he continued to speak as though she was just a chance-met colleague. 'Can I get you something to drink?' he offered politely, 'or would you rather go straight through to the dining-room?'

'Straight through, please,' Maria confirmed calmly and raised her chin a notch even though his cold civility felt like a rebuke. 'If I don't get something to eat soon I'm going to start gnawing on a table-leg.'

The creases beside Leo's eyes deepened briefly as

he gave a short laugh. 'That makes a change. It wasn't long ago you weren't eating enough to keep a sparrow alive.'

'It's amazing the difference it makes to your appetite when you know the food is going to stay with you when you've eaten it,' Maria explained wryly as he held out her seat for her, his manners impeccable in spite of the strained atmosphere between them.

On the surface the meal went well. The food and service were excellent and, providing they spoke of medical matters, the two of them were never at a loss for conversation. But underneath the politeness Maria could feel the tension building.

When she couldn't help yawning for the third time, nearly spilling the cup of tea she'd chosen instead of the coffee she'd rather have had, Leo rose to his feet.

'Time for bed,' he prompted avuncularly as he offered her his hand to help her out of the comfortable armchair she'd taken root in after their meal.

Maria's heart leapt stupidly at his words until she mentally dragged it under control again, reminding herself that there was nothing salacious in his pronouncement.

Even so she couldn't help the wistful daydream that teased her mind as he escorted her into the lift and up to their room.

If, instead of a sham, this had really been their honeymoon would he still be standing there in the ornate glory of the lift with a careful six inches between them? Would he merely take her elbow to guide her along the eccentric steps and turns of the corridor or would he have put his arm around her shoulders?

While her thoughts had been meandering they'd

reached the door of their room and he was opening it, pushing the dark polished wood wide with one hand while he pocketed the key with the other.

'I'm going to have another cup of coffee before I come up so there's no need to hurry with the bathroom.'

He'd turned away as he began speaking and was already part-way along the short corridor before Maria realised that he wasn't coming into their room with her.

She watched his retreating figure with stunned amazement and his long strides had taken him as far as the corner which would take him out of sight before she hastily managed to find her voice.

'Leo,' she called softly, mindful that there might be others already settled for the night in the nearby rooms. He paused momentarily to glance at her over his shoulder.

'Yes?'

'Goodnight,' she whispered into the silence that stretched between them, her heart in her mouth as she waited—hoping to hear him say that he'd be back before she went to sleep.

For a long moment he stood wordlessly, his eyes brooding and shadowed in the subdued light of the corridor.

Finally, 'Goodnight,' he echoed, and disappeared, leaving her to close the door on the last of her fragile hopes.

CHAPTER EIGHT

LEO was as good as his word. He'd said that he was going to organise a job-sharing scheme which St Augustine's would accept and he'd done it. The only trouble was that Maria found it impossible to limit herself to the part-time work she was now expected to do.

'What are *you* still doing here? You should have gone home an hour ago.'

Maria jumped when Peg's voice sounded behind her and she swung round to face her.

'I've just finished a session with Julie Turton's parents and grandparents. I think I finally managed to get through to them that they're actually doing her harm when they give her ''special treats'' of biscuits and sweets to ''make up'' for becoming diabetic.'

'Poor kiddie,' Peg murmured as she busied herself pouring boiling water into the tiny teapot she kept ready on a tray in the corner. 'I've lost count of how many times they've had to rush her in with a hyper since she was diagnosed. You'd think no one had explained it all to them the way they ignore all the rules and advice.'

'That's why I had them come in together this afternoon,' Maria said tiredly as she used both hands to brush the straggly wisps of hair away from her face. 'I thought if I went over it again with all of them in the same room they would all know that they were getting

136

the same information and had to obey the same set
of rules.'

'But they had you in there for over an hour and a
half and you've come out looking like a limp dishrag,'
Peg began militantly as she advanced on Maria like an
avenging angel with only a steaming cup of tea as a
weapon. 'Anyone would think the hospital didn't have
any trained counsellors the way you take on the
stubborn ones.'

'Don't you start lecturing me again, Peg Mulholland,'
she said as she sank gratefully into the chair and, ignoring the saucer, wrapped her hand around the proffered
cup. 'I'll be fine as soon as I've had this tea.'

'Providing you don't take your bottom out of that
seat for at least the next half-hour when you've finished
it,' Peg replied trenchantly, her look as severe as her
tone. 'You might have got away with overworking
when I didn't know about the baby. . .'

Maria groaned. 'I wish I'd kept my big mouth shut,
now. I'd have had several fewer weeks of persecution.'

'That's another thing,' Peg jumped in. 'How on earth
did you get to seven months without anyone noticing
you were pregnant? In an ordinary office I could understand it but even in a hospital where we're supposed
to be trained observers no one had a clue.'

'Partly it was because I lost so much weight in the
early stages with morning-, noon- and night-sickness.
Then it took me a long time to put it back on. . .'

'But you've got a real football-sized lump there,
now.' Peg nodded towards Maria's recently non-
existent waist. 'You can hardly say that *that* looks like
a hernia!'

'Hardly!' Maria chuckled helplessly, nearly spilling

her tea. 'But being a doctor does help—we get to wear this voluminous white camouflage outfit.' She picked up the edge of her coat to show what she meant and the stethoscope started to slide out of the pocket.

'Oops!' She made a grab for it but missed. 'I can't move quite so fast nor fold up quite so far in the middle these days,' she said ruefully as she accepted the offending article from Peg. 'I'm beginning to feel quite bloated.'

'In comparison with a stick-insect,' Peg retorted rudely, glancing down at her own far more rounded figure. 'You should try battling with my inches. At least yours will all disappear once junior arrives.'

'With any luck.' Maria crossed her fingers then a sly smile crept over her face. 'Anyway, what are you complaining about? I have it on good authority that a certain handsome doctor is rather smitten with you—curves and all. Hospital gossip has it that he's flown over from Italy three times in as many weeks just to see you.'

'Rubbish!' Her friend turned away swiftly but not before Maria had seen the tide of colour staining her cheeks. 'He came over to attend the presentation that Leo did for the lecture series.'

'And the other times?' Maria taunted.

'Oh, hush!' Peg flounced towards the door. 'You sit quietly and finish your tea.'

'Yes, Sister. Of course, Sister,' she mocked with a grin as she toasted the rapidly retreating back with her cup.

She sighed deeply once Peg had gone and let her head drop back to rest against the high back of the chair.

Now that she was alone she could admit just how

tired she really was. She'd thought that job-sharing with Leo would have taken the pressure off her but it almost seemed as if it had made things worse.

Ever since they'd returned from their weekend away he'd been at great pains to treat her like fragile china. More often than not she'd get ready to go into the hospital and find that he'd ordered a taxi to take her to work and when her duty was over and he came to take over for her there would be a taxi waiting to take her home again.

The time they actually spent together was minimal; in the last few weeks it had been barely more than the time it took to hand over responsibility for the patients.

It was the off-duty times that she found most difficult. If they were both home at the same time their conversation seemed to be confined solely to medical topics, almost as though they were afraid to loosen the tight hold they had on the situation.

When each evening had finally dragged until they were both yawning and bed was the only option, Maria found herself clinging desperately to the edge of the mattress in an attempt to stay on her own side of the bed.

She was disgusted to note that Leo didn't seem to find any difficulty in falling asleep, his breathing growing deep and even within minutes of his head touching the pillow.

Night after night Maria watched the numbers on her alarm clock click monotonously around while she remembered the first night they had spent in each other's arms and each time her eyes sheened with tears as she compared it with the nights they'd spent together since.

The first night of their 'honeymoon' had passed

without so much as a memory to hold on to.

After a brief tussle with her self-consciousness she'd finally donned the silky nightdress Peg had given her, grateful for the concealing folds as she slipped nervously between the crisp cotton sheets.

Remembering Leo's pleasure in threading his fingers through her hair, she'd deliberately left it loose, innocently expecting it to invite his attention when he returned to their room.

Unfortunately, before he arrived the events of the day had caught up with her and the next thing she'd known was a knock on the bedroom door as room service delivered her breakfast on a tray the next morning.

The times when she was at home alone weren't any better.

After the frantic activity involved in moving her belongings into his new flat halfway between their two hospitals she found that she couldn't settle to anything and the thought of trying to catch up on her sleep when he wasn't there was laughable.

She'd tried it once, lying down in the centre of the bed early one evening with a light blanket over her legs. Several attempts at courting sleep, following the methods taught at her prenatal relaxation classes, had been no help.

Trying to find a more comfortable position had her rolling over onto her other side but with her first deep breath she drew in the unmistakable mixture of soap and male musk which told her that she was lying on Leo's pillow and all thought of sleep fled.

Finally she had decided that her only alternative, if

she was to retain her sanity, was to keep busy at the hospital.

She sighed heavily as she reached out one hand to deposit the empty cup on the corner of Peg's desk then paused to gather her thoughts.

It had taken some careful arrangement but she was slowly managing to fill the empty hours by scheduling appointments such as the meeting this afternoon with Julie Turton's family. When she had been working a full timetable it would have been impossible to spend such a long time with them but, in spite of the fact that she felt exhausted, she honestly felt that she had achieved something this time.

'What are you still doing here?' a familiar deep voice demanded as Leo entered the room. 'The taxi was supposed to have taken you home a couple of hours ago.'

'That's just what Peg said and in exactly the same tone of voice,' Maria told him, her words covering the leap in her pulse which happened every time she saw him.

'Well, we're both right. You shouldn't be spending so many hours on your feet.'

'I've been sitting down for most of the afternoon,' she said self-righteously.

'In between walking from floor to floor and bed to bed with a couple of forays to interview rooms and intensive care,' he detailed all-too-accurately.

'Peg's a rotten sneak,' she muttered sulkily. 'I'm taking good care of myself. My last check-up was perfect.'

'Apart from a slight rise in blood pressure and too little weight gain.'

Maria blinked in surprise. She hadn't realised that

Leo knew that she'd been for her regular visit to the antenatal clinic, nor that he'd made a point of finding out about the state of her health. The thought that he'd bothered shocked her into silence and made her feel all warm inside.

'Come on, Dr da Cruz. Time to go home.' He walked over to stand in front of her and hold out both hands, towering over her as she sat in the chair.

Tentatively she placed her own in them and saw their pale slenderness disappear in his broader palms as they touched for the first time for so long.

As she'd lain awake in the darkness she'd often wondered if she'd imagined the electricity in the contact between the two of them but she hadn't. Pulling her out of the soft upholstery was a mundane occurrence but it had her pulse racing and her breathing irregular enough to suggest that she'd been using the stairs instead of the lift all day.

'Ready?' he prompted when she didn't move, her feet apparently glued to the floor.

'Oh. Yes. I've got my bag. . .' Her voice trailed away in surprise when he placed a solicitous arm around her waist to usher her towards the nearest bank of lifts. In silence she revelled in the unaccustomed contact, hoping that it might signal a change in the atmosphere between them.

It wasn't until they were waiting for a lift to arrive that she saw a couple of the junior nurses nudging each other and smiling that she wondered at his actions.

Suddenly her heart sank as she realised that the staff grapevine would expect such things from the couple who had married after such a whirlwind romance. Obviously Leo was making certain to provide the show.

With all her pleasure in his display of concern gone she waited stoically until they were out of the building before she turned slightly so that his arm would slip away, her pride forcing her into conversation.

'How was young Steven in intensive care? Any progress?' She was referring to their latest emergency patient. 'Did anyone find out what had happened to him?'

'According to his older brother he'd run away to hide from a group of bullies and made the mistake of trespassing on a building site. Apparently there was an old house in the process of being demolished to make way for a new development and part of a wall collapsed on him.'

'That explains all the cuts and bruises all over him, poor kid.' Maria winced as she remembered the dozens of cuts and grazes and the depth of some of the bruising. 'Why didn't the building company make sure this sort of thing couldn't happen? If it's dangerous surely the site should be made secure from trespassers?'

'It's an ongoing problem, apparently. It doesn't matter how carefully a site is boarded up children and squatters always seem to find a way in.'

'You didn't say whether he'd made any progress yet?'

'Not so far. He's obviously still heavily sedated until we get another scan and find out if his brain is still swelling.'

'So it could be days or even weeks before his poor family know what permanent damage he's suffered. . .'

As ever when they were talking about the patients they had in common there was no lack of conversation between them but by the time Leo was parking the car in his designated space by the flats they'd grown silent, the tension once more like a living presence between them.

Maria had gathered her belongings together and was already swinging her legs out of the car door by the time he reached her.

'Here, let me help.' He held out one hand towards her.

She longed to accept his assistance and just an hour ago she would have done. Not just because it helped her to avoid the struggle of getting to her feet but also because she enjoyed what she had thought were little displays of consideration

Except they weren't, were they? she thought, angry at her gullibility as she disregarded his outstretched hand and scrambled out unaided. It was all display and precious little consideration—for her feelings, at least.

She marched self-righteously up to the door and across the entrance hall towards the flat, totally ignoring his presence beside her.

'I'll unlock the door for you,' he offered as he flicked through the small bunch of keys to select the correct one.

'I'm perfectly capable of unlocking a door,' Maria snapped pettishly as she opened her bag to get her own keys out and promptly dropped the contents all over the floor.

Cross with her own clumsiness, she tried to stoop swiftly to gather everything up again but there was an unexpected argument between her knees and her expanding waistline. For several seconds she flailed her arms wildly, trying to regain her balance before she collapsed in an ungainly heap at his feet.

'Maria! Are you all right?'

He was there instantly, his strong hands lifting her effortlessly to her feet and turning her around as he checked her for any signs of injury. 'Did you hurt yourself?' he demanded, his brows drawn together over his patrician nose as he frowned. 'Let's get you inside quickly and I'll take a proper look at you.'

'It's all right, Leo. You can relax.' Maria forced the words out through the constriction in her throat. 'There's no one here to watch the show.'

' "Show"?' he repeated coolly, taking a step backwards in the face of her refusal to be helped. 'What are you talking about?'

'Oh, come on! We're both reasonably intelligent people.' She finally found her key and twisted it viciously in the lock before she flung the door wide and marched in. 'We both know the *real* reason why we got married and while it makes good PR to act like the caring husband when we're surrounded by our colleagues you hardly need to keep the charade up for *my* benefit.'

She dropped her bag disdainfully on the coffee-table in the middle of the understated elegance of the living-room and the catch burst open, spewing her belongings out all over the floor for the second time.

'Dammit!' She swore through gritted teeth as she stood staring down at the mess, blinking furiously to hold back the threat of tears.

'Maria. . .'

'Don't!' she cut him off, whirling away from his approaching figure to stare out at the fading light, her arms wrapped defensively around her ribs. 'Don't say anything. I'm not in the mood to put up with a lot of. . .'

'Maria. Stop it.' His hands grasped her shoulders and he spun her back to face him, the speed of the movement rocking her back on her heels so that she had to clutch at his arms to steady herself.

'What's going on?' he demanded, his eyes boring deep into hers as she felt the first betraying tear spill onto her cheek. 'What on earth's got into you today?'

'N-nothing.' She sniffed and opened her eyes wide in a futile attempt at stopping any more tears falling. 'It's just. . . You didn't. . .' She gave up the attempt with a shake of her head.

'That's not good enough.' He gave her a little shake. 'You accused me of playing charades and I want to know what brought that on.'

'Well, it's true, isn't it?' She glared defiantly up at him. 'Today, in the hospital, you were playing the caring husband escorting his wife for an audience of nurses.'

'If you want to put it like that, I suppose I was,' he agreed tightly and she watched his lips draw into a narrow disapproving line. 'Of course, it didn't occur to you that I *am* your husband and I might actually *want* to care for you, did it?'

'Why should it?' She tilted her chin up. 'I'm nothing to you, except the woman who was in the wrong place at the wrong time and ended up pregnant with a baby you don't want.'

'That's not true!'

'Ha! Which part?' she challenged. 'Can you deny that you wanted me to get rid of the baby? Can you deny that until Andreas told you I wasn't a prostitute he'd paid for you'd forgotten all about me?'

'Yes.'

The forceful whisper cut through her tirade like a scalpel blade, stunning her into silence.

'Yes,' he repeated, his steely grey eyes intent on her. 'I *do* deny that I'd forgotten about you. You never left my mind.'

'If that's true why did it take you three months to come looking for me?'

'Because I didn't know how to make contact. . .'

'Oh, *please*!' she said in disgust. 'You knew who I was the very next morning at the conference. If I was so memorable you could have walked straight up to me and introduced yourself.'

'So could you,' he retorted. 'This is the nineties. You were just as much at liberty to approach me— after all, you did the night before.'

'But I didn't know who you were. I didn't even know I was in the wrong bed. . .'

'How was I supposed to know that?' he said, his logic infuriatingly correct. 'You appeared in my bed, made earth-shattering love with me and then didn't so much as speak to me the next morning. What was I supposed to think?'

'Oh, God!' Maria covered her face with her hands to hide her embarrassment. 'I never thought about how it must have appeared to you. . .' She sighed. 'So that's why you glared at me in disgust.'

'Glared at you?'

'While you were eating. You were staring at me across the tables and you glared.'

'The only reason I glared was because I had just been told I had to cut my time at the conference short. I'd been planning on finding out about you—where you came from and why you were forced to supplement your income in such a way.'

'Supplement my income. . .!' she gasped, her hands curling into vicious-looking claws. 'You. . .'

'Shh!' He clasped his own hands over hers and brought them up to his chest where he cradled them against his warmth. 'I know it isn't true—in fact I think I knew it long before Andreas told me he'd had nothing to do with your presence in my room.'

'Then, why. . .?'

'I couldn't forget you,' he said sincerely. 'I couldn't forget what you'd done for me that night when I was so depressed and had no one to turn to.'

'But I didn't do anything. I only. . .' She blushed, quite unable to continue, and shuffled uneasily from one foot to the other. Finally she stepped away from him so that he had to release his hold on her hands and perched herself on the edge of the settee, reaching out to switch on a small table lamp in a vain attempt at distracting him.

'Ah, Maria, if you only knew,' he murmured as he joined her and coaxed her into leaning back more comfortably. 'You brought life and light into my soul at a time when I thought there wasn't any left in the world.' He stroked one hand over her dishevelled hair then cradled her hot tear-stained cheek against his shoulder. 'You were sweet and lovely and you seemed to know exactly how I was feeling—how desperate and depressed.'

'Oh, Leo, I was feeling the same way too.' Her expression was wry at the memory of that day and she rubbed her face against the fine fabric of his suit jacket just to enjoy the sensation of being so close to him. 'It was the sort of day that makes you question why you ever became a doctor in the first place and then you were there, as warm and comforting as a log fire in a cold world.'

'You were wrong, you know.' He tilted her face towards his insistently. 'I *do* care about you; I wouldn't want you to get hurt.'

Maria's heart leapt at the sincerity in his tone, her pulse beginning to race. Did he mean that his feelings for her were deepening? Was he, too, starting to fall in love? Was he going to tell her. . .?

'I can't forget that I should bear the major part of the blame for your pregnancy,' he continued, his eyes darkening with self-reproach as his arm tightened around her shoulders. 'I should have remembered to take some sort of precautions for the sake of my *own* safety, never mind yours.'

'Well, if you believed my *profession* made it likely that I could be carrying VD or HIV, or whatever, why didn't you?' Maria demanded shakily, stiffening against him as she realised with a sickening jolt that his only driving force was guilt.

'I'll admit that partly it was the brandy I'd had. I don't drink much, as a rule, and it was potent stuff but it was also because I wanted to believe that what was happening was all just a beautiful illusion—the sort of erotic fantasy that every man dreams about.'

'Do they?' Maria couldn't help the unwilling fascination in her voice. This was a topic she'd never discussed before—barely even thought about in her drive to achieve, to excel.

'What do you think?' His voice had grown husky and a darker hue appeared in the lean planes of his cheeks and he looked away from her curious gaze for a moment.

When he met her eyes again there was a different expression in the depths of his, almost as though he was lost in his memories, and Maria held her breath, a strange electric excitement running through every nerve as she waited for his deep husky voice to continue.

'I turned over in the darkness and found a sleek, naked body in the bed beside me, all soft and warm with a mane of silky hair spread out across the pillow.' He paused for a moment as his eyes travelled over her face, his fingers rising to release her wild curls from their customary bondage.

'It was too dark to see you but my hands transferred a picture directly into my mind as I ran my fingers through this abundance.' He suited his actions to his words, spreading her hair out across her shoulders like a mantle.

Maria shivered, awareness of his touch spreading right through her body.

'Then, when you turned sleepily into my arms and our bodies met for the first time. . .' his words faltered gruffly, as though he was unaccustomed to speaking about his feelings '. . .it was sheer heaven and I never wanted to wake up. . .'

Silence fell in the room but this time there was no rough edge to it, with Maria trying desperately to find something innocuous to talk about. This time she was perfectly content to stay just where she was, surrounded by Leo's strong arm with her head resting on his shoulder. This time she knew that whatever happened between them they had managed to open up lines of communication and would be able to talk about it.

At one point Leo insisted that she stayed put on the settee while he went out to the kitchen and microwaved a potato each to go with the cold meat and salad waiting in the fridge but as soon as their meal had been cleared away he put on some more of the soft piano music that had accompanied their meal and rejoined her on the settee.

She hadn't realised just how long they had been sitting there until her eyes began to grow heavy and she glanced down at her watch.

'It's getting late,' she said regretfully, not wanting this magical interlude to end. 'And you're due in the hospital tomorrow morning.' She angled her head so that she could look up at him without having to lift it from its comfortable position and for the first time was able to examine his face at close quarters.

'You're looking tired,' she said sadly, recognising that the stress of their situation had been taking its toll of him, too, in spite of the fact that he seemed to have been sleeping so well.

'I'm not surprised.' He pulled a wry face. 'I've only just finished my lecture tour; I've got a couple of papers I'm trying to edit ready for publication and, on top of that, I'm job-sharing with my wife and not getting a lot of sleep.'

'*You*'re short of sleep?' Maria demanded in amazement. 'You must be joking! You drop off as soon as your head hits the pillow. I can hear your breathing alter.'

'Ha!' Leo's laugh was dryly ironic. 'I might have fooled *you* into thinking I was sleeping but I can't fool my body or my brain. I'm shattered. . .'

Maria chuckled. 'What a pair of idiots,' she commented as she began the increasingly arduous business of getting out of the soft upholstery. 'I think we both need our heads knocked together.'

'Better than that.' Suddenly Leo's hands were there to pull her to her feet. 'I think we both need a good night's sleep. I don't know about you but I feel as if a great weight's been lifted off me.'

'Yes.' Maria stood for a moment while she explored her feelings. 'I really feel as if I'll be able to sleep tonight.'

As always, Leo ceded the bathroom to Maria first and she made her way towards the bedroom as he carried their empty cups out to the kitchen.

She was too tired and too relaxed to do much more than stand limply under the shower, her hair wound up inside a protective towel so that it didn't get wet. She'd taken to wrapping herself up in Leo's spare towelling robe for the transition to the bedroom, changing into her nightdress while he took his turn in the bathroom so that she was tucked safely out of sight under the covers before he reappeared.

She realised that tonight was different when she walked into the bedroom swathed in his robe to find a midnight-blue slither of silk draped across her pillow.

Her eyes flew over him as he lounged back against the headboard. He seemed perfectly relaxed, his jacket gone and his unbuttoned shirt gaping open casually to reveal his broad, darkly furred chest, his long legs crossed at the ankle as he stretched out lazily on the bedspread.

Finally their eyes met across the width of the room and she knew that he could read the question in her own dark honey depths without a word being spoken.

'I never saw you wear it,' he murmured huskily, one lean hand reaching across to trail sensitive fingertips over the delicate fabric. 'Peg told me she'd packed it for you but. . .' He shrugged.

'Why would Peg tell you about my nightdress?' She felt herself grow pink at the thought of Leo discussing her nightwear with another woman—even her friend, Peg.

'Why wouldn't she when I asked her to get it for you?' he replied simply and she was delighted to see the teasing glint in his eyes directed at her at last.

'What did you do—ask her to choose something she thought I'd like?' Maria was intrigued.

'No.' He paused as though debating whether to say any more then continued, almost bashfully. 'I'd actually seen that one in a window and I thought it would suit you but the shop wasn't open at the time. I just told Peg where it was.'

For a moment Maria was thrilled at the thought that he wanted her to wear the nightdress he'd chosen for her but then she remembered how different her shape was from the first time he'd seen it and hedged shyly.

'As long as you don't expect me to model it for you,' she stipulated. 'I'm not exactly lithe and lissom any more.'

He shook his head as he slid his legs off the bed and straightened up to his full height, walking towards her with a gentle smile on his face. 'But still very beautiful,' he murmured persuasively as he stopped right in front of her.

'I *mean* it,' Maria warned him sternly, a smile trying to lift the corners of her mouth at his blatant attempt

at changing her mind. 'I'll wear the nightdress if you
want me to but I'm not putting it on until you take
yourself off to the bathroom.'

He pulled a face but Maria was sure it was just for
show as he muttered, 'Spoilsport,' on his way to the
shower.

She finished her own preparations for bed, sliding
the deep blue silky fabric over her pale powder-dusted
skin before she settled into her own side of the bed.
She smiled in lazy amazement at the changes that had
occurred in the last few hours, hardly able to believe
that she and Leo were the same two people who had
driven away from St Augustine's in such an icy
atmosphere.

For the first time she actually believed that the two
of them might develop a friendship strong enough to
sustain them through the tensions of the next few weeks
and, who knew, even beyond.

The bathroom door opened and Maria's heart
stumbled frantically as Leo stepped into the bedroom
with nothing more than a towel wrapped around
his hips.

Suddenly she realised that it was the first time since
their abortive honeymoon that she'd actually *seen* him
in their bedroom. Ever since she'd moved into his flat
she'd made certain that the light was turned out by the
time he finished in the bathroom and that she was
settled onto her side, facing away from the door.

'What big eyes you've got,' Leo teased and Maria
flushed as she realised that she was staring at him, her
eyes helplessly travelling over him, admiring the lean
muscular power of his chest and thighs. Her hands
clenched reflexively at the memories of what the dark

whorls of body hair felt like to her fingertips.

'D-do you wear p-pyjamas?' she heard herself stammer and wished that she could disappear into thin air when Leo laughed delightedly.

'No, I don't wear p-pyjamas,' he mocked gently, one hand reaching for the tucked edge of the towel.

'Oh!' Maria gasped, turning away rapidly when she realised that he was about to remove his towel, then listening with feverish intensity to the rustling sounds as he lifted the covers on his side of the bed and slid in behind her.

'It's safe to look now,' he taunted her gently when the mattress stopped moving.

'Don't want to,' she said, trying to sound aloof but only managing to sound like a disgruntled child.

'Ah, Maria,' he chuckled and she felt the bed move again as he turned towards her, his voice continuing from right beside her ear. 'Sometimes it's hard to remember that you're a fully trained doctor—you get embarrassed so easily and you rise to the bait so fast when I tease you.'

She could feel the warmth of his breath on her shoulder, the thin spaghetti strap doing little to conceal her shiver of awareness as he stroked the tendrils of curly hair away from her neck.

'Are. . .are you going to turn out the light?' she faltered. 'It. . .it's getting late and. . .and. . .'

There was a long silence behind her before she heard the rustle of bedclothes and the click of the switch that plunged the room into darkness.

'Goodnight.' His words emerged on a tired sigh and Maria was suddenly afraid that her shyness and inexperience had destroyed all the progress they'd made this evening.

'Leo?' she whispered tentatively, her heart feeling as if it would jump out of her throat it was beating so hard.

'Yes?'

The unadorned word was without expression and she could only hope that she had found her courage in time.

'Would you. . .?' She swallowed, her mouth suddenly so dry that she could hardly speak; could hardly force out the words she needed so badly to say. 'Will you. . .hold me?'

Her heart sank when the silence in the room went on and on with no sign of movement and no reply.

Finally she heard the sound of a deep inhalation and his taut murmur, 'Are you sure?'

For a second she was fighting the tears that burned behind her eyes at the aching echo of emptiness in his voice. It was the realisation that he was just as prey to loneliness and uncertainty as she was that drew the word from her.

'Please. . .'

CHAPTER NINE

Leo's arms were still cradling her possessively against the warmth of his body when she woke up early the next morning and for the first time since that night in Italy she felt absolutely content.

'Good morning, sleepyhead,' a deep voice rumbled up from the depths of the chest she was using as a pillow and she tilted her head to look up at him shyly in the pearly morning light.

'Good morning,' she echoed. 'How did you know I was awake?'

'I thought you might be when you started stroking me.' He glanced down towards his chest and Maria froze when she realised that her fingers had been rhythmically smoothing over the dark pelt between his flat male nipples.

'I'm sorry,' she gasped, snatching her hand away. 'I didn't realise I was. . .'

'Come back here.' He grabbed her hand and replaced it exactly where it had been. 'Don't stop—I was enjoying that.'

'Oh!' She ducked her head as memories assailed her of the way she had explored his body once before and she marvelled at how fearless she had been then and how timorous now. Surely it couldn't all be a result of her pregnancy—the knowledge that although she was still enthralled by the magnificence of his body her own was less attractive to him.

157

'What's the matter?' He coaxed her chin up with one hand until she had to meet his eyes.

'I'm. . . You're. . . Isn't it time you were getting up?'

'Ah, Maria, you're so sweet and so transparent!' He leant down to plant an unexpected kiss on her parted lips then retreated again until he could watch her face, smiling at her as she felt a blush steal up from her throat.

'Now. Tell me what's worrying you,' he demanded. 'You might as well because I'm not letting you out of this bed until you do.'

'But. . . You're joking!' she laughed. 'You've got to go on duty this morning.'

'Just think how guilty that will make you feel— that you were solely responsible for me not turning up on duty because you wouldn't tell me what's bothering you.'

His nonsense was sufficient to break the tension just enough for her to speak about her fears.

'You look just the way I thought you would,' she burst out, her eyes flashing down to where her pale hand was spread out against the perennial coppery tan of his chest, the dark furring of his silky hair curling up between her fingers. 'Even better than I imagined,' she added candidly.

'Thank you,' he said gravely and she was grateful that he didn't tease her, his eyes holding hers steadily as he waited for her to continue.

'It's just. . .I'm *not*. The way I was, I mean,' she added at last, the words emerging in a jumble as she tried to unravel her thoughts. 'You look so good. . .' she gestured wordlessly towards his sleek, fit body with one hand '. . .and I'm all. . .' she grimaced.

'And you're all. . .what?' he prompted. 'All beautifully lush and ripe with your glorious hair rich and shiny and your skin glowing with health?'

'Hardly,' she objected. 'I'm over seven months pregnant!'

'And you're still the sexiest woman I've ever seen,' he growled as he tipped her away from him to lie on her back. 'Your body has a timeless slender elegance which will look just as good in thirty years as it does now and your pregnancy does nothing to detract from it.'

Maria snorted her disbelief.

'You honestly don't understand, do you?' He sounded amazed. 'You don't realise that the taut curve of your belly over the baby and the extra fullness of your breasts is a blatant advertisement of your fertility and an aphrodisiac for the man responsible for your condition.'

'But they're heavy and cumbersome,' she objected as she tried to pull the sheet up over herself. '*I'm* heavy and cumbersome.'

'Not to me,' he said quietly as he gently released her tight grip on the edge of the sheet and drew it away from her.

She watched in nervous embarrassment as his eyes travelled over her body and saw them linger on the recently acquired bounty of her breasts like a physical caress and she was startled to see her nipples react as though he had actually touched them, tightening so that the silky fabric of her nightdress outlined their proud crests.

'Ah, Maria,' he groaned. 'Your body is just as responsive as I remember.' He stroked the betraying

peaks with the tip of one finger and she arched helplessly towards his hand.

'Leo,' she whimpered. 'You can't. . .we can't. . .'
She stopped on an indrawn breath as he cupped one
breast in his hand and anointed her with his tongue
before he blew softly on the clinging fabric. The sudden
chill tightened her nipple still further, making her long
for his mouth again.

'But you want to,' he murmured persuasively as he
trailed his fingers up the slender length of her thigh,
gathering the hem of her nightdress as he went. 'You
want to see if it feels as good as you remember when
I stroke your satiny skin and when you find out that it
feels even better than you remember you'll want to
find out how much else will be better still.'

'But Leo. You. . . Ahhh. . .'

'You see,' he encouraged as he cupped her intimately
and she surrendered, powerless to resist his skilfully
arousing fingers and the equally arousing murmur in
her ear. 'I told you it would be better than ever. . .'

Maria found herself filled with a new confidence in
the following few weeks and she finally recognised in
herself the 'glow' of pregnancy she'd scoffed at when
she was being so sick.

She'd resigned herself to the fact that she was soon
going to have to stop work entirely but, with Leo's full
agreement, she'd promised her 'special' patients that
she would be calling in to visit them when they came
for their regular transfusion sessions or when, God
forbid, they had a 'crisis'.

Her heart had lightened when she'd seen how much

more relaxed Leo had become over the traumas of their young charges.

His skills as a physician had never been in doubt but it was his old burden of guilt over his son's death which had caused the destructive scarring on his soul.

Now Maria was looking forward to the birth of their child with a new assurance that, whether the baby had the misfortune to inherit beta thalassaemia disease or the good luck just to carry the trait, she and Leo would be able to cope with it together.

She smiled secretively as her thoughts strayed to the special gentleness he had brought to their lovemaking as her pregnancy grew more advanced, always more concerned with her enjoyment than taking his own pleasure.

'You've got that soppy grin on your face again,' Peg's voice interrupted her thoughts and Maria was fiercely glad that she couldn't *read* them as well.

'You mean the soppy grin like the one you get when you hear that Andreas is on his way to England again?' Maria retorted, not to be outdone.

'Huh!' Peg flounced over to the kettle in the corner. 'With a little more effort you could become really insufferable. When am I going to get rid of you for a while?'

'I'm due in about four weeks now,' Maria confirmed, 'so I could have started my maternity leave a fortnight ago but I've been so well. . .'

'That you decided to stay on and make my life a misery,' Peg completed for her and they both laughed with the ease of long friendship.

'Seriously, though. What have you got for me today, Peg? Any problems crop up in the night?'

Suddenly Peg, too, was all business.

'We've had one little mite transferred to us this morning from intensive care. She was badly savaged by a neighbour's dog.'

'She's still being specialled?'

'Until she settles down with us and you're happy with her obs,' Peg confirmed. 'I've put Dawn with her. She's got the experience and she's calm enough to cope with panicky parents.'

'Any others you want me to take a look at?' Maria slid herself forward in her seat preparatory to heaving herself upright. There was still little obvious evidence that she was so far through the term of the pregnancy and many of the other staff had no idea that there was a baby due at all.

As far as Maria was concerned her little passenger almost seemed to have doubled in size and weight in the last couple of weeks, making her usual energetic suppleness a thing of the past, so she'd be glad when the waiting was finally over. . .

'We've got a new one of your ''special'' children.' Peg smiled as Maria's attention was caught. 'The family have recently come here from abroad—staying with relatives.'

'What form are we dealing with? How much history have they brought with them?'

'It's another beta thalassaemia and they don't seem to have much information about her treatment. I don't know whether they just didn't bring it with them or what.' Peg put the new file on top of the small pile and handed them to Maria.

'Right, then. Let's start with Rashna Besharati,' she said decisively after she'd read through the sparse information available. 'Are her parents with her?'

'Her mother and an aunt, if you're lucky, because mum is Gujarati and doesn't speak any English and the aunt acts as interpreter for them.'

'In that case, if she isn't here we'll have to get one of the volunteer interpreters up here. Gujarati is Kumar's speciality, isn't it? Can you find out if he's on duty today?'

'Will do,' Peg confirmed as they made their way into the ward.

In the event they found just one visitor beside Rashna's bed and had to wait until Kumar was found to interpret for them.

Maria had to content herself with smiling a lot while she checked the listless little girl over and read through the notes in her file so far.

When Kumar finally arrived there was another wait while he conducted a rapid-fire conversation with the frightened-looking woman who compounded the problems by bursting into tears.

'What on earth's going on, Kumar?' Maria was only just beaten by Peg when she stepped forward to comfort the woman. 'What did you say to her to get her into such a state?'

'It's not me,' he denied with both palms held out towards her. 'She was talking to me about her daughter's illness and she let slip that she and her husband engineered this visit to her sister to try to get help for the girl. Now she's afraid that we'll make them leave without any treatment.'

'Please, tell her that the rights and wrongs of her presence here are nothing to do with me,' Maria directed. 'I'm a doctor and I'm here to try to help Rashna.'

It was obvious that her calm words and reassuring smile had already begun to work their magic even before Kumar had finished translating them and Maria was showered with a torrent of grateful thanks.

'Please make sure she knows that I don't know how much I'll be able to do for Rashna. She's in a pretty bad way.' Maria sat down on the edge of the bed and picked up the little hand not connected to drips and stroked it gently.

The young woman's eyes turned to Maria as Kumar spoke, their liquid darkness filled with sorrow as she spoke again.

'Mrs Besharati asked me to tell you that she has already lost one child this way and just when she has been told that she is carrying another, Rashna has become so much worse.'

'Ask if she's had any tests done to show whether the baby she's carrying has the same illness?'

The ensuing conversation was fast and furious, neither of them allowing the other time to finish a sentence properly before they began speaking again.

Finally Kumar reported back.

'She says she didn't know that such a test could be done. Apparently she lives in a very rural area where medical attention is sparse and they couldn't afford to go to the nearest city for such things.'

'Well, before you go, will you get one of each of the leaflets in Sister's office. You'll find a set in Gujarati published by the Thalassaemia Society in London. In the meantime, her home situation explains why Rashna is in such a bad way. She's very anaemic and jaundiced;

her legs are ulcerated and her spleen is huge.' Maria's hands were moving gently over the apathetic child, pointing out each of the features as she spoke about them.

Kumar was translating her words carefully, holding up a hand at intervals to halt Maria when Mrs Besharati needed clarification.

'Her bone marrow has been hyperactive and this has caused thickening of the cranial bones,' she continued. 'If we were to take X-rays we'd probably find she'd suffered pathologic fractures.' She paused while Kumar translated, watching the sadness deepen on the young mother's face as he catalogued the problems.

Maria began again, knowing that a mother who had already lost one child would understand all too clearly the implications of what she was about to say.

'According to the case history she's had just enough blood transfusions to keep her going but the resulting build-up of iron has been deposited in her heart muscle and that is what's causing her heart to dysfunction.'

Maria watched the mother's narrow shoulders slump even as she tried to smile at her daughter and Maria knew that she was prepared for the worst to happen.

By the time Leo arrived on the ward to take her home all Rashna's test results were back but in spite of the fact that she was hooked up to the complete panoply of what western medicine could do for her condition she hadn't shown any improvement.

'It's not that I don't trust the rest of the staff to look after her,' Maria murmured as she stood holding the rail at the end of Rashna's bed. 'It's just that I hate to go while she's in such a bad way.'

When Leo's hand covered hers in a gesture of

support she was filled with a feeling of warmth.

'We could always treat ourselves to a meal in town,' he suggested. 'Then we could call back in to have a look at her before we go home.'

'You're sure you don't mind?' Maria smiled gratefully up at him, loving him all the more for his understanding nature.

'Of course not. I know you'd only be sitting at home worrying about her.' He accompanied her to collect her few belongings and escorted her out to his car.

'There's a little Italian restaurant not far away,' she suggested. 'It wouldn't take long to walk there.'

'I think you've done quite enough walking for one day, pregnant lady. Remember our agreement? You're only staying on at work as long as your obstetrician is happy with everything. If you go and get yourself over-tired you'll be back home and off your feet so fast. . .'

'All right, all right! I'll get in the car,' Maria submitted hastily, laughing impishly up at him as she settled into the plush leather seat.

In spite of the light-hearted mood at the beginning of the meal the two of them gradually grew more sombre as they discussed Rashna's prospects for recovery until neither of them could eat any more.

The poor waiter was upset by the amount of food they had left on their plates and when they refused even to look at the sweet trolley he was devastated.

'I feel so guilty,' Maria muttered out of the side of her mouth as she and Leo slunk quietly out of the restaurant. 'He looked as if he was going to cry when you wouldn't even have a coffee.'

'We'll have to make sure to starve ourselves for a

week before we go there again so we can do the food justice,' Leo suggested as he unlocked the car doors.

They were both silent on the return journey to the hospital and Maria was very conscious of just how much Rashna's situation must remind Leo of his own son's illness.

'You don't have to come up with me,' she suggested when they arrived in the staff car park. 'I only wanted to look in on her for a minute.'

'So do I,' he said sombrely, 'just in case there's anything I can think of that might help. . .' His voice died away and they both knew what he was thinking about.

'Any change in Rashna's condition, Ian?' Maria demanded hopefully when the first person they saw when they reached the children's ward was the registrar coming out of Sister's office.

He shook his head wordlessly, his grim expression needing no further explanation.

'Damn,' she heard Leo mutter explosively and she surreptitiously reached for his hand and threaded her fingers between his to hold on tight.

'How is her mother coping?' Maria's heart was heavy with sympathy. 'You did know that this is her second child to go this way?'

'Yes. I saw the note on the file,' Ian Stanton confirmed. 'God, I hate this feeling of helplessness. . .'

There was a sudden commotion inside the ward with the shrill sound of a monitor and the swift passage of feet.

'Quick!' Maria whirled towards the door and released the catches to allow them entry.

'It'll be her heart.' Leo's voice was clearly audible

over the swish of curtains and the clang as equipment was swung into position and one part of Maria's brain registered that he sounded very calm—almost too calm.

Mrs Besharati had backed away from her daughter's bedside when the medical staff descended on her and Maria put a consoling arm around her slender shoulders as they watched the frantic activity together for a moment.

She stiffened when she saw her daughter's pale body arch up off the bed as they tried to restart her heart, a gasp of distress leaving her throat at the savage sight.

She grabbed Maria's hand and started speaking rapidly, her eyes full of tears as she shook her head in denial.

'They're trying to make her heart beat again,' Maria said, her words slow and clear as she tried to mime over her own heart what was happening.

When the poor woman only became more agitated Maria wished that there was someone—anyone—who could translate for them to save her having to do so much guessing.

'Mrs Besharati, please. . .' Maria grasped hold of both of her hands and turned her away from the bed where her daughter lay. 'Can you tell me what you want?' She made eye contact with her and slowly began to mime—first, that her daughter's heart started beating again and her eyes opened and then that Rashna's heart stayed silent and her eyes stayed closed.

'Yes?' she questioned at the end of the pantomime and the young woman nodded her understanding before she copied Maria's mime for Rashna's eyes opening and followed it with a shake of her head, then mimed her heart staying silent and nodded her head—while the tears streamed down her cheeks.

'Leo? Ian?' Maria called but the two of them were so intent on what they were doing that they barely heard her. 'Leo,' she repeated louder. 'Please, listen. Mrs Besharati wants you to stop.'

For a moment the two men were so still that the scene around the small child's bed was almost like a posed tableau then, at a nod from Leo, Ian continued the interrupted heart massage.

'Are you certain?' Leo was the first to find his voice. 'How did she tell you that? She doesn't speak any English and you certainly don't know Gujarati.'

'Watch,' Maria said and touched the woman's elbow, gesturing for her to repeat her mime.

There was a simple dignity to the young woman as she stood beside her child's bed with tears streaming down her face and showed them that she didn't want them to fight for her daughter's pitiful life any more.

'That's enough, Ian.' Leo's voice was gravelly as he touched the registrar on the shoulder. Ian had been watching the by-play while he automatically maintained the little child's circulation but at Leo's direction he lifted his hands away and stepped back.

Leo reached across to pull the sheet up to Rashna's chin and Maria saw the slight tremble in his hand when he gently smoothed several straight, dark strands of hair away from her forehead before beckoning the child's mother to make her own farewells.

Maria didn't know what had woken her but it was still dark outside. It wasn't until she went to turn over that she realised that Leo wasn't beside her in the bed.

She listened for a minute but when she couldn't hear any sign of movement in the flat she began to worry.

He'd been very quiet when they'd driven home from the hospital and she'd tried to let him know that she was there for him if he wanted to talk but even when they'd gone to bed he'd been silent, holding her in his arms with a quiet desperation.

Knowing that she wouldn't be able to go back to sleep until she had reassured herself that he was all right, she donned the silky wrap she'd bought to cover her burgeoning shape and padded out towards the kitchen.

The whole flat was in darkness so she had no idea where he might be until she walked into the lounge and felt his presence.

'Leo,' she whispered softly, not wanting to wake him if he'd accidentally fallen asleep in his reclining chair.

A slight flash of movement drew her eyes to the settee and then she saw the darker shape of his head and shoulders outlined against the pale upholstery.

'You should be in bed,' he murmured gruffly into the darkness. 'Did I disturb you?'

'I don't think so. I woke up and you weren't there so I came to see if you were all right.'

She heard his deep sigh in the darkness, her hearing somehow more acute because she couldn't use her eyes.

'I couldn't sleep,' he admitted at last when she had grown accustomed enough to the darkness to see him shrug. 'I was thinking about that little girl this evening.'

'Rashna,' Maria murmured in confirmation of her fears. She had known that Leo must be hurting inside as all the painful memories of his son's sad life were resurrected.

She shivered as her body began to lose the heat from the bedclothes and wrapped her arms around herself.

'You're getting cold,' he commented disapprovingly. 'Go back to bed. I'll be all right.'

'Will you come with me?' she appealed. 'I won't be able to go back to sleep, knowing you're out here and. . .and I need you to warm the bed up again.'

She heard his brief huff of laughter. 'I knew I had my uses,' he murmured as he straightened up and came towards her. 'Do you want me to get you a drink?'

'I'd love one but I'd be dashing backwards and forwards to the bathroom if I have anything now.'

She felt as if the silent battle was half won when she heard him following her into their bedroom and she slid quickly into her side of the bed.

He was slower to get in, sitting silently on the side of the mattress for several minutes before he finally discarded his robe and joined her under the covers.

'Do you want to talk?' Maria said into the darkness when it was obvious that neither of them was ready to go to sleep. 'Perhaps it would help if you tell me what you're thinking . . .'

He was silent for a long time but Maria felt that she knew him well enough now to know that he would only speak if and when he was ready. All she had to do was be patient.

'She's expecting another baby,' he said suddenly, his voice taut with suppressed tension. 'She'd already lost one child and her second one was desperately ill but she's going to have a third. . .'

The mixture of anguish and disbelief in his voice made it necessary for Maria to swallow hard before she could speak.

'Perhaps she and her husband are hoping that they'll be lucky this time—that the percentages will be on their side for a change. Perhaps they think it's worth the risk. . .'

'But what if it's a *third* child with beta thalassaemia? How could they bear to go through it all over again?' he burst out. 'It's the bloody uncertainty of it all. How can they bear the uncertainty. . .?'

For the first time Maria regretted her decision not to have any tests done when it was the right time to find out about their baby. She just hadn't imagined when she'd made the decision according to her own feelings and beliefs that it would have such an effect on Leo.

'I'm sorry, Leo,' she whispered through a throat full of tears as she turned towards him. 'I didn't realise. . .'

CHAPTER TEN

MARIA felt guilty.

The more she thought about it the more she realised that she should at least have considered Leo's point of view when he'd first heard about the baby.

Once he'd told her about the loss of his son to the same set of circumstances as surrounded her own child she should have had the sensitivity to understand that he was going to spend the remaining months of the pregnancy under enormous pressure.

'It's the uncertainty. . .' she repeated, hearing the anguish in his voice when he'd said it.

Oh, it had been easy enough to steel herself against his appeals when he was a stranger but now that she loved him the guilt at her blind obstinacy was taking its toll on her.

'If there was only some way to turn the clock back so I could have the tests,' she murmured into the emptiness of the lounge as she knitted furiously, her needles moving as fast as her thoughts. 'Or if there was some way of finding out now without risking the baby. . .' She sighed, knowing that she could mutter and wish as much as she liked for the rest of the pregnancy and it wouldn't make any difference to the outcome.

The saddest part about the whole situation was that just as she and Leo should have been drawing closer together in preparation for the arrival of the baby they

were being pushed further and further apart by his
tension and her guilt.

'It was Rashna's death that brought it all to a head,'
she said aloud, needing to hear the words that had been
circling inside her brain for the last fortnight. 'On the
surface it seemed as if everything was all right but
underneath. . .'

The telephone shrilled and she saw several stitches
slide off the point of the needle as she dropped the
knitting on the table beside her seat.

'Dr da Cruz?' Maria frowned as she heard the voice
on the other end. It sounded familiar. . . 'This is Kumar
at the hospital.'

'Yes, Kumar.' She recognised his voice now. 'What
can I do for you?'

'Do you remember telling me to give the Gujarati
leaflets about foetal testing to Mrs Besharati?'

Did she remember? Of course she remembered.
She'd done little else but think about the whole episode
ever since it happened.

'I remember,' she agreed calmly. 'Is there a
problem?'

'No problem, except she's desperate for you to be
with her when she has the foetal blood sampling done.'

'Me?' Maria was startled. 'But she hardly
knows me.'

'She says she trusts you,' he replied. 'You took the
trouble to find out what she wanted to say and made
the doctors listen.'

'But what about her family? They. . .' For a moment
Maria was going to continue her objections but then
she remembered that the two of them might share a
far deeper kinship than the poor woman did with her

sister-in-law. A bond of inheritance.

'When is she booked to have the test? Has she been given a date yet?'

'She's here now,' Kumar said, his tone slightly harrassed. 'She wouldn't let them proceed until I'd spoken to you.'

'Oh, Lord!' Maria glanced down at her watch and calculated travelling times. 'My husband isn't home yet so I'll have to get a taxi. Hopefully I'll be with you in half an hour.'

With Kumar's assurances that he'd let everyone know she was on her way, Maria pressed the button to disconnect the call and pressed another one that Leo had programmed to dial the local taxi company automatically.

She just had time to don a clean maternity smock and comb her hair into some sort of submission before the taxi arrived, only remembering just as she was about to pull the door closed behind her that she hadn't left a note for Leo.

'Gone to St A's,' she scribbled on the message pad beside the phone. 'Obs and Gyn Dept. Foetal blood sampling.'

She dropped the pen, conscious that time was passing but couldn't resist picking it up to add a final message.

'Love you,' she scrawled, knowing that it was the first time she had ever dared to let him know how she really felt about him. For a second her courage nearly failed her and she was tempted to scribble over the words but in the end she let them stand. Perhaps letting him read it first was the coward's way but it was time she told him the truth.

*   *   *

The obstetrics and gynaecology wing was a little world all of its own—a strange mixture of calm waiting and frantic activity staffed by a special breed of people.

Here everyone was linked by a common purpose—to help women conceive healthy children and bring them safely into the world.

Maria smiled wryly as she sat beside Azra Besharati. No one had batted an eyelash when she'd arrived in the department, thinking that she was just another one of their expectant mums. It was when she donned an over-size gown to accompany the frightened woman that they looked askance at her—until she produced her hospital credentials and explained the special circumstances surrounding her presence.

This time it was one of the midwives who offered to translate for them but it seemed to be enough for Azra that Maria was with her.

By the time the procedure was completed and Azra had been told when to return for the counsellor to discuss the results with her it was several hours since Maria had left her hurried note for Leo.

She knew that it was common for him to arrive home late and had regretted not being able to catch him at the hospital to cadge a lift home but there was always the possibility of a taxi for the return journey if Leo didn't turn up.

In the distance she'd heard the ululating wail of several ambulances and knew that there must have been a nasty accident somewhere in the catchment area of St Augustine's. She spared a thought for the poor souls involved and hoped that she wouldn't be hearing about any of them from Leo after his next spell of duty.

She was just making her way out of the department

on her way to the bank of telephones in the main reception area when she heard the muted buzz of the telephone at the nurses' station.

'Dr da Cruz?' a puzzled voice called after her and she let the door close again as she made her way back towards the young nurse. 'I don't know if I got the message right but there was a man on the other end who told me to tell you not to do anything. Just wait until he arrives. He said he was Dr da Cruz.' She frowned in her confusion until Maria laughed and explained.

'Dr da Cruz married Dr Martinez so now they are Dr da Cruz and Dr da Cruz.'

'Well,' the young woman laughed. 'I only hope you don't both work in the same department or everyone would be confused.'

'We do,' Maria told her, and they laughed together.

'Did my husband give you any idea how long he'd be? Did he say where he was?' She glanced down at her watch, wondering when she would ever get a chance to eat this evening.

'He's down in the accident department,' she volunteered. 'There was a big accident on his way to the hospital. . .'

'Oh, my God,' Maria breathed in horror. Her heart thumped heavily with shock as she remembered the sound of all those sirens. Leo had been on his way to fetch her and he'd been involved in an accident. . .

Suddenly she was running, her feet flying over the smooth expanse of the corridor in spite of her ungainly bulk, the frantic sound of the nurse's voice lost in the urgency to see Leo; to find out how badly he was hurt; to see if there was anything she could do for him; to tell him face to face that she loved him.

The lift seemed to be moving in slow motion, stopping at every floor while people took their time about getting in or getting out until finally she couldn't stand it any more and pushed her way swiftly past a group of chattering youngsters to make for the stairs.

There was a strong sense of déjà vu as she made her way towards the emergency department via the echoing stairwell but never before had she felt such urgency.

She was quite breathless by the time she arrived and had to pause a moment before she could speak.

'The accident victims who came in a little while ago. Where is Dr da Cruz?' she demanded shakily.

'And you are?' the receptionist queried.

'His wife,' she said, feeling a new sense of pride in saying the words aloud. 'Also Dr da Cruz.'

'Oh. Well, in that case I suppose it's all right to let you go through.' She looked dubiously at the pretty smock which only partly camouflaged Maria's swollen body. 'One of the mens' gowns should fit you.'

To be perfectly honest Maria couldn't have cared if she'd been told to dress up as Father Christmas as long as she could see Leo.

As soon as she was through the staff-only doors she grabbed a gown and was forcing her hands into the sleeves as she walked towards the trauma rooms.

'Maria?' Leo's husky voice came from behind her and was full of disbelief. 'What on earth are you doing down here?'

'Leo!' She whirled to face him, her heart in her mouth as she looked for his injuries, but. . . 'You're not hurt!' she exclaimed with delight, her eyes running over his green-clad figure with relief.

'Why should *I* be hurt? I only stopped to help—I was first on the scene and followed the wounded in.'

'But. . .you sent a message up saying you'd been in a big accident on your way to the hospital!'

'Oh, God, sometimes this place is worse than playing Chinese whispers in a maze,' he muttered while he reached up to release the ties on his gown. 'Come on, let's go. They don't need me any more. . .' He stuffed the gown in the laundry bin and sent hers to join it, his voice suddenly clipped. 'I don't think you should be charging around like this after what you've been through this afternoon.'

'Oh, Leo,' she smiled up at him, almost floating with the euphoria of relief. 'I'm all right now that I know you weren't one of the injured.'

'That wasn't what I meant,' he retorted grimly as he gripped her elbow and ushered her along the corridor towards the main entrance. 'I was talking about *your* message.' He stood back to allow her to precede him through the door then continued briskly across the parking area towards his car.

Maria hurried to keep up with his much longer strides, hardly daring to ask him to slow down. He seemed to be so angry. Had it been her admission on the note which had upset him so much? Had she spoiled everything?

'Dammit!' He stopped in his tracks, swinging her to face him. 'What on earth made you do it? It's only two weeks until it's due. Where was the sense in risking everything?'

'I didn't take any risks,' she objected, mystified by his strange mood. 'I phoned for a taxi to bring me here and I've been sitting down for most of the afternoon.'

'That's *not* what I mean and you know it,' he muttered through gritted teeth as he grabbed her elbow again and thrust her towards the car. 'You were so dead set against it so what on earth made you decide to have it done now?'

'Do what?' Maria demanded as he unlocked the doors and glowered at her until she gave in and slid into the seat, grateful for the support when her knees began to quiver with delayed reaction.

'It's my fault, isn't it?' he continued as soon as he joined her in the car. 'It's because I let you know how hard it was living with the uncertainty. That's why you went to have the test done.'

Maria felt her jaw drop open with amazement when she finally realised what he meant.

'No!' She shook her head. 'You've got it all wrong.'

'Oh, you needn't spare my feelings,' he interrupted, obviously not listening to her. 'I've been an idiot and I realise it.'

'Yes, you're an idiot,' she agreed, changing tack in an effort to make him listen to her and it worked, his eyes darting to meet hers when his words stopped.

'You *are* an idiot if you think I'd risk our baby like that.'

'But. . .your message. . .'

'Another version of Chinese whispers, I'm afraid. And this time it's *my* fault.' She explained about the phone call and spending the afternoon keeping Azra Besharati company. 'I never thought you'd read the message and believe I'd gone to have the test done on *our* baby.'

'Oh, God, thank you.' The whispered words were like a prayer as his eyes closed and he dropped his head back wearily against the headrest, seemingly drained by the relief of tension.

'Leo?' she said, tentatively putting her hand on his arm.

'Shh.' He covered it with his own and rolled his head to fix her with a steely, intent gaze. 'No more talking until I get us home. All right?'

She was silent for a moment while her eyes travelled over his face, searching for the hurt and anger which had filled it just a short while ago but they were gone without a trace.

'Yes,' she said through a weak smile of relief. 'Let's go home,' and she settled back into her seat.

The journey was over in no time and they had hardly got as far as the sitting-room before Leo was pulling her into his arms.

'Oh, Maria,' he breathed into her hair as he held her tightly. 'I'm sorry I didn't trust you. I should have known after the fight that you put up before that you'd never do anything to risk the baby.'

Maria closed her eyes to savour the sensation of holding her husband in her arms after the fright this afternoon. She'd been so afraid that just as she found the courage to tell him that she loved him he was being taken away from her.

'I wrote the note in a hurry,' she said, pulling back to look up at him when she finally managed to get her brain working again. 'The taxi was waiting outside to take me to the hospital and I didn't have time to phone you but I didn't want you to arrive home in my absence and not know where I was.'

'And I turned jumping to conclusions into an

Olympic event,' he admitted, guiding her towards the settee.

When he'd drawn her once more into his arms and settled her head on his shoulder he continued, his voice a deep velvety purr beside her ear.

'All I could think about on the way to the hospital was that you'd never have thought of doing it if I'd talked to you—told you what I'd been thinking.'

'But you did. . .' she began, her objection ending when he put one finger to her lips to silence her.

'If I'd told you that I finally understood what you meant about it all being worth the risk. If I'd told you that I trusted you; that I knew that if our baby *was* born with beta thalassaemia disease you would never neglect it the way Sophia did. . . Dammit! I should have told you that I love you!'

'Only if you mean it,' Maria whispered through quivering lips, wondering how much joy she could stand before she simply exploded with it.

'Of course I mean it!' He sounded stung that she could doubt him. 'I think I started to fall in love with you when I turned over in bed one night in a hotel in Italy and found a naked, long-haired nymph beside me who set the world on fire and brought me back to life.'

'Ha!' she scoffed. 'You thought I was some sort of over-sexed courtesan.'

'No.' He shook his head and smiled gently. 'Not once I met you. You were too innocent-looking, too sweet for that.'

'So soft that you thought you could bully me into doing what you wanted?' she reproached him with the memory.

'Thank God you turned out to have a core of steel.'

He tightened his arms around her. 'Otherwise I'd never have had an excuse to get you to marry me.'

'You didn't need an excuse,' she said simply. 'All you had to do was ask. . .' She stopped with a gasp.

'Maria?' He drew back a little to look down at her. 'What's the matter?'

She held her breath for a moment then released it slowly, concentrating on the new sensations inside her body before she glanced at her watch.

'Maria?' he prompted. 'Talk to me. What's the matter?'

'I'm sorry, Leo,' she smiled up at him wryly. 'I know you've been going backwards and forwards all day but would you mind driving the car again?'

'You want to go for a drive?' He was mystified. 'I thought we were going to have a quiet evening at home?'

'So did I,' she agreed, 'but it appears the baby has other ideas.'

'The baby. . .? Oh, my God, the baby! It's early. . .' He leapt off the settee as though he'd been shot from a gun and ran agitated fingers through his hair. 'Where did I put the keys? Have you got your case packed? Can I do anything to help?'

'Yes. You can calm down,' she laughed. 'Your keys are in your right hand trouser pocket where you *always* carry them and my case has been packed for weeks. Now all you have to do is get me on my feet—I feel like a beached whale!' She held both hands out to him so that he could haul her upright.

'Oh, Maria, what did I ever do to deserve such luck?' he breathed as he pulled her up and wrapped his arms around her. 'If you hadn't climbed into my bed that night. . .'

During the long hours that followed they had time to talk.

For the first time Maria felt comfortable asking him about his son. She knew, now, that over the last few months Leo had gradually been coming to terms with the tragedy of his short life and his own part in it.

This time, instead of guilt and anger, she heard joy and love in his voice as he talked about Nico's impish sense of humour and the way he would always greet his father with a hug.

'Did you have any idea that you and Sophia had beta thalassaemia trait?'

'*I* didn't. Not until she tested me after he'd been diagnosed.'

'*She* tested you?' Maria queried in surprise, vaguely remembering that he'd mentioned it before.

'Being a haematologist, she said she would be able to short-circuit the usual rigmarole,' he explained. 'If I remember rightly Theo heard what was going on and that was when she persuaded him to be tested at the same time. . .'

Maria felt a prickle of unease but couldn't put her finger on it immediately and by the time her next con-traction had ended she'd forgotten about it, the midwife telling her that she was in transition and it would soon be time to start pushing.

'At least,' she panted a while later as she rested for a few seconds between bouts of mind-boggling effort, 'we know that St Augustine's will be testing this baby as a matter of course.'

'Yes.' He wiped her face gently with a cool damp cloth and then held her hand again, his support unwavering. 'This one will be taken care of from the moment it's born.'

Suddenly things started moving very quickly and it seemed as if it was only minutes before Leo tenderly passed her a tightly wrapped little wrinkled bundle.

'A girl,' Maria breathed, dragging her eyes away from the tiny features to gaze mistily into Leo's tear-filled eyes. 'Oh, Leo, she's perfect. Look. . .' and she offered their baby up to him.

'If she's anything like her mother she's bound to be perfect,' he murmured huskily as he stroked one hand over the tiny head. 'Just as she's bound to be beautiful and kind and caring. . .'

'And if she takes after her father she'll be bossy and self-confident and kind and caring. . .' She reached out one hand to cup his cheek and drew him towards her for the kiss that would complete the circle.

'Oh, Maria, thank you for fighting me,' he said, his voice sounding almost rusty. 'Thank you for sticking to your guns, otherwise this day would never have happened.' He gazed at her with clear grey eyes, their warmth soothing and healing and without a trace of the old hurt and bitterness.

'If it hadn't been for you,' he continued, 'I would never have had the courage to try again, not once I knew that it had been my fault that Nico died.'

'It took two of you with the trait to produce him,' Maria reminded him and she had a momentary flash of the venom in Sophia's face when she'd cornered her at the wedding reception and warned her not to get pregnant.

Maria had been moved into the ward, her bed beside the windows with a view out over a small rose garden when it happened again—as though her subconscious was trying to tell her something.

Suddenly the unease that she'd felt whenever the topic of Sophia came up grew into a nasty suspicion and she carefully composed a question in her mind before she spoke.

'When Sophia ran the tests did Theo test positive?' she asked, keeping her tone casual.

'No.' Leo pulled a face and looked down at the hand he was cradling between his own, one finger tracing the delicate gold band she'd chosen to wear. 'I always thought that was why Sophia married him—because he could give her children without the fear of them inheriting anything more than the trait.' His tone became musing. 'Actually, I was surprised that they didn't start their own family straight away.'

'I'm not,' Maria said candidly as everything suddenly became clear and watched the shock enter his eyes. 'Theo's not happy with her because he doesn't love her. He knows she's only interested in the lifestyle he can give her.'

'How can you possibly know that?' Leo objected. 'You only spoke to them for a minute or two.'

'Call it feminine intuition if you like but I'd like you to do something for me.'

'What?' he blinked at the apparent change of topic.

'Have yourself tested for beta thalassaemia trait,' she challenged.

'Is that a joke?' he demanded with a frown as he straightened up out of the chair beside her bed. 'I told you, I've already been tested. . .' His voice faded away as the implications of her request sank in.

'Oh, my God,' he breathed and sat down again, hard. 'You think she switched the results.'

'It would certainly explain the hold she has over Theo,' Maria suggested. 'She'll never need to lift a finger all the while she's married to wealthy Theo da Cruz and he'll never get rid of her all the time she's threatening to tell his brother that the baby wasn't his.'

'Poor Theo,' he murmured. 'I knew she wasn't happy when I insisted I wasn't going to be the figurehead for the family holdings—that's always been Theo's strength in spite of his apparent laziness. If she set her sights on him as my replacement he probably didn't stand a chance. It was just everybody's bad luck that she got pregnant—with such tragic results for poor Nico caught in the middle.'

'You realise what this means, don't you?' Maria demanded with a wicked grin.

'Uh-oh,' Leo murmured. 'Why do I think I'm going to regret asking?'

'I'll tell you, anyway,' she said sweetly as a bubble of joy began to swell inside her. 'If, as we suspect, your test shows that you *aren't* positive that means that none of our children can suffer from beta thalassaemia disease. The most that can happen is that they inherit the trait.'

'And?' he prompted warily.

'That means there's no reason why we shouldn't have as many children as we want,' she declared triumphantly.

'Oh, God.' Leo sank his head in his hands, his elbows propped on the edge of the mattress. 'It's only minutes since she gave birth to the first baby and she's already planning a houseful!'

'Leo. . .?' Maria touched his head with a tentative hand. 'We don't have to have any more if you don't want to. It's just. . .every time I see you with children it's obvious how much you love them. . .'

When her voice trailed away miserably he lifted his head from his hands and she could see his face.

'You rat!' She tightened her fingers in the thick silk of his hair and tugged. 'I thought you were upset and didn't want any more children and there you are grinning like the Cheshire cat.'

'Ow!' He lifted her hand away and rubbed his scalp. 'Leave me some hair! I'll be pulling my own out soon enough if we end up with a house full of children.'

'A house full?' she questioned with longing in her eyes as new hope blossomed into life.

'Whatever the tests show,' he confirmed. 'As you said, each pregnancy for a couple who both carry the trait has a one-in-four chance of the baby having the disease but you've taught me to realise that it's a three-in-four chance that they won't. And if I'm clear. . .' He shrugged easily.

He captured both of her hands and leant forward to pin them on the pillow, either side of her face.

'I love you, Maria,' he murmured as he hovered protectively over her. 'For now, for always.'

'For now, for always,' she echoed, her heart full to overflowing as she gazed up into eyes that radiated happiness. At last the bitterness and pain had disappeared without a trace and she offered her lips to him to seal their pledge.

Return this coupon and we'll send you 4 Mills & Boon Medical Romance™ novels and a mystery gift absolutely FREE! We'll even pay the postage and packing for you.

We're making you this offer to introduce you to the benefits of Reader Service: FREE home delivery of brand-new Mills & Boon Medical Romance novels, at least a month before they are available in the shops, FREE gifts and a monthly Newsletter packed with information.

Accepting these FREE books and gift places you under no obligation to buy, you may cancel at any time, even after receiving just your free shipment. Simply complete the coupon below and send it to:

MILLS & BOON® READER SERVICE, FREEPOST, CROYDON, SURREY, CR9 3WZ.

No stamp needed

Yes, please send me 4 free Mills & Boon Medical Romance novels and a mystery gift. I understand that unless you hear from me, I will receive 4 superb new titles every month for just £2.10* each postage and packing free. I am under no obligation to purchase any books and I may cancel or suspend my subscription at any time, but the free books and gifts will be mine to keep in any case. (I am over 18 years of age)

M6JE

Ms/Mrs/Miss/Mr _____

Address _____

_____

_____ Postcode_____

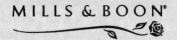

MILLS & BOON®

Medical Romance™

Books for enjoyment this month...

THE REAL FANTASY	Caroline Anderson
A LOVING PARTNERSHIP	Jenny Bryant
FOR NOW, FOR ALWAYS	Josie Metcalfe
TAKING IT ALL	Sharon Kendrick

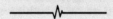

Treats in store!

Watch next month for these absorbing stories...

THE IDEAL CHOICE	Caroline Anderson
A SURGEON'S CARE	Lucy Clark
THE HEALING TOUCH	Rebecca Lang
MORE THAN SKIN-DEEP	Margaret O'Neill